The Anniversary Box

To Laura—

Live to just(?),

Thank you!

Tim

The
Anniversary Box

Tom Murphy

Encircle Publications
Farmington, Maine U.S.A.

Book design and cover design: Eddie Vincent
Cover illustration © Shutterstock

Published by:
Encircle Publications
PO Box 187
Farmington, ME 04938

Visit: http://encirclepub.com

Sign up for Encircle Publications newsletter and specials
http://eepurl.com/cs8taP

To my brother, Dan

"There are cracks in everything,
that's what lets the light in."

—Leonard Cohen

Chapter One

Peggy Moore walked into the hardware store on 7th Street in Garden City with a task not on her official to-do check list. It was six weeks before her wedding, which she had been anticipating with excitement beyond words since she was a little girl, but now had a bit of trepidation.

"Can I have a two-foot section of garden hose, please," she said to the clerk behind the counter, a bald man in a flannel shirt.

"I hope you're not planning to strangle somebody."

"I'm going to use it as a teaching tool with my fiancé at dinner tonight."

"Teaching tool?"

"Enlighten him on the finer points of male consciousness to earn an 'I do.'"

The man chuckled before cutting a section of tubing from a spool at the end of the gardening aisle. He walked back to the register to ring her up. "Store policy, once we make the cut we can't provide a refund."

"I see store policy and marriage align."

He laughed. "After thirty-one years, I'm sure my missus will tell you I skipped a class or two. Need a receipt, young lady?"

"No, thank you."

"Good luck with your pupil tonight."

She gave him a wink as she walked out the door with her section of hose.

Peggy had met her fiancé Michael on a golf course during a charity outing two years earlier, shortly after moving to New York. He was on the sixteenth hole, coming toward her from the left. She was on the third hole which ran parallel to the sixteenth fairway where he had pulled his second shot. She had hooked her drive, which put their two shots in the same vicinity in the rough between the two fairways.

As they approached each other, she noticed he was cute with wavy black hair. Whenever people asked them how they met, he'd describe this moment, and how he couldn't stop staring at her... that she was gorgeous in her short, flowered-print skirt, accenting her "hundred-watt smile, and thoroughbred legs."

As they drew close to their two golf balls lying side by side, he said. "What are you hitting?"

"Titleist 2."

"Me, too."

They looked down at the two balls, both were Titleist 2s.

"One's in a hole, the other is sitting up. Why don't

you hit the one sitting up? You'll have an easier shot out of the rough," he said.

"You'd do that for me?"

"I will, if you'll have a drink with me at the end of the round."

"But you're on the sixteenth hole. I'm only on the third. That's a long wait."

"I've been waiting an eternity for you," he said. It sounded like one of those lines guys give girls that start out "Did it hurt?" And when you say, "Did what hurt?" the guy says, "When the angels dropped you to earth." But he was cute with a cocky self-confidence, and a tight butt, so she was happy to say yes.

They saw the world differently; he was a "T" she was an "F," according to the Myers-Briggs personality scale. When told that studies showed some people live to be one hundred years old, despite poor eating habits, while others who take care of themselves die early, he characterized that as, "Some win, some lose." She, on the other hand, believed that it was unfair how the vicissitudes of life are parceled out unequally, or as Leonard Cohen expressed it "even a radish screams when it's pulled from the ground."

"We're a perfect match," she said. "You're head, I'm heart."

He was an accountant with a rising career. Analysis was his stock-in-trade. She was an up-and-coming marketing exec with a social media start-up on Long Island. She lived by her "antennae," which is how she described her wits that allowed her to navigate the treacherous waters of business. She liked that he was athletic, since she had been a champion track and cross-country runner in high school. They would go on week-long bike trips, the kind where a van brought the luggage from inn to inn. Their lovemaking at night after a full day of biking was nothing short of out of this world. On one trip, they found themselves on a lonely stretch of road in mountain country in Idaho. He pointed to an area beyond a patch of trees and invited her to meet him in "yonder field" for what he called "canoodling."

"The bike people, they'll be waiting for us."

"Will you marry me?" he asked.

"What?"

"Just wanted to see if I could get your attention."

"You're crazy."

"Crazy about you."

She joined him, and now had canoodling heaven in her memory bank along with the certainty that this was the guy she wanted to marry one day — for the spark he brought to her life.

Over time, she came to regard their different takes on the world as similar to negative and positive poles of a magnet. Put negative and positive together, and presto. The two magnets bond, which is what they

did most of the time. But switch one pole around —
negative pole to negative pole — and the magnets
repelled each other. That's what had been happening
a lot lately, a spike in negative-to-negative push backs.

The disagreements had become more frequent
as their wedding date drew near. His parents were
deceased, as was her mom, and her dad was in a
nursing home following a stroke. She was twenty-
three years old, he was twenty-seven. Both had
fledgling careers, no family — neither had siblings
— and not a lot of money. They were paying for the
wedding themselves, and it was not surprising that
tensions would arise over expenditures.

The row that night had started small.

She had prepared chicken marsala, which she
needed to reheat in the oven since he was late
coming over to her place. She should have known
the ground was shaky when he walked in without a
bottle of wine, which was "his job." She poured two
glasses of tap water and set them and the already-

plated chicken marsala on the table, and they sat down to eat. She made a comment about lint on his sweater, and he responded that he was working very hard at the office to pay for "my share of the wedding" and thus couldn't be aware of every little piece of lint that attached to him.

"You're not paying attention to big things as well as small things."

"Oh, really? Name me one big thing I have been neglecting,"

"Me!" she said.

White showed on all four sides of his eyes, and thus, the first shot in a new wedding-planning skirmish had been fired. It wasn't long before he brought up the "fur coat issue."

"Have you put that silly idea about the fur coat picture aside?"

The fur coat picture was a photo she wanted very badly for their wedding album. She envisioned a shot of her with her bridesmaids in fur coats gathered under a big tree. It was impractical — six bridesmaids and the bride sporting bad-ass poses in fur coats and showing leg — but it was something she wanted, and he had complained often about the expense not just to pay the photographer extra to take the photo, but renting the coats.

"Several of my friends have their own fur coats," she said as she reached for her purse and moved it to her lap, fingering the section of hose she had purchased at the hardware store.

"But what about the ones who don't own coats?"

"It's not a lot of money to rent a fur coat for a day."

"You're going to need more than one fur coat."

"It's a small thing."

"It's money we don't have."

That's when she took the hose out of her purse. He looked puzzled, so she had him where she wanted him.

"You call it money. I call it memories."

"What are you talking about?"

She used the hose as a prop and showed him how money to cover expenses for the wedding went in one end of the hose and came out the other end as memories. "But if you crimp it here," she said, and she squeezed the hose closed in the middle, "you don't get memories, you get zilch!" She congratulated herself not just for thinking up the metaphor but anticipating the need to use it — and buying the hose.

That's when the escalation started.

"What about your student loans?"

Oh no. He wasn't bringing that up again! She had taken out $160,000 in student loans during college and had a monthly payment of $2400 against them. It was more than she wanted, but her mom had been sick with lung cancer while she was in school, and her father, a self-employed educational consultant, could not work because he had to care for her mom. Normally, her dad paid for her schooling, but she saw the strain he was under, so she took an initial loan for $25,000. Over the next three years, as her mom's illness worsened and expenses for her dad expanded to tsunami proportions, she upped the total to $160,000.

"I wish you wouldn't keep bringing that up. I was helping my dad."

He took the section of hose out of her hands and spoke like a teacher addressing a slow pupil. "I admire that, but loans go in this end, and if payments don't flow out this end, debt collectors come calling."

"I am taking care of them. I will take care of them. I would never want you to take care of them." She was stammering. It's what she did when confronted with facts she couldn't deny despite believing she had them under control.

"When I'm married to you, I'll be married to the loans. Most important, you never told me the total amount until six weeks ago."

"I'm taking care of them, I told you."

"Tell that to the bankruptcy judge. Student loans

are not covered in bankruptcy court if you default. They will garnish your wages, *our* wages."

And that's when he said the word that broke it all apart, tore apart all they had built in two years. He said, "You deceived me."

She was insulted. She was hurt. She was infuriated. Most of all, she felt crushed, as if the ceiling had collapsed on her.

"Did you just say I deceived you?"

"You never told me how huge the loans are."

"I told you I was taking care of them. And you choose a word like 'deceive?'" Her eyes were suddenly ablaze, like a California wildfire.

"I wish you could understand my point of view."

"It's not your point of view I need to understand. I understand perfectly your point of view, which is why I'm about to explode. When people get married, it's a case of one plus one equals one. Each has to trust the other."

"What are you talking about, one plus one equals

one? That's not even proper math."

"It's an expression I learned from my parents, who loved each other very much. When people get married, each individual, a 'one,' commits to join with the other, another 'one.' When they commit to each other fully, the two become one. One plus one equals one. My parents called it their Gift of the Magi Principle."

"I never read that story in high school."

"Obviously, which explains why you have no capacity to support me. The Gift of the Magi Principle was the cornerstone of their marriage, and it needs to be the cornerstone of any marriage I will be part of."

"Look, it's simply the size of the loans," he said, and he reached into his shirt pocket for a pad and pen to calculate compound interest and prove his point. She reached across the table and grabbed the pad. She tore the page, balled it and tossed it at him, hitting him square between the eyes. Had the page been a bullet, it would have been time to price out column inches in the newspaper for his obituary.

"Oh, no, not that stupid hose again!" he said as she took the tubing and stretched it into a straight line.

"Listen up, pal, because I'm going to show you what you need to know if you expect me to marry you. Love flows in one end, and when love is real, it flows out the other end like out of a fire hose, and it nourishes the relationship." She folded the hose in the middle, pinching it closed. "But you have crimped your hose; you have cut off life and love — and thus, you have cut me off. I can't marry a man who crimps his hose."

"You're blowing this all out of proportion, honey. Look, I love you! Okay?"

"Don't give me empty words. You have pinched your hose closed, cut me off, and that's what your actions tell me loud and clear. You don't support me! To say 'deceived'!"

Her heart was beating fast; her hands were sweaty. Time passed in a blur. Suddenly he got up, placed his napkin on the table, and headed for the door.

"My chicken's cold, and I need air," he said, and he let the door slam behind him on the way out.

She got up from her seat and stepped to the sink, not for any purpose, but because it offered a place to stand and steady herself.

It took a few minutes, but her head stopped spinning, and she realized she had the piece of hose still in her hand. She tossed it into the wastebasket with a solid thrust, and it landed clean like Stephen Curry hitting a shot from mid-court.

Then as she stared at the basket rocking back and forth from the impact of the hose, she realized she had not just thrown away $4.19 she had paid for the hose. She had tossed away two years of time, energy — and love — on someone without any capacity to give back emotionally on the investment of heart she had made in him.

And the store didn't do returns.

Chapter Two

"Ping!" It was a sound that made her heart jump in the morning.

The soaring little note on her phone meant a rise-and-shine text from Michael awaited her, a sweet greeting to start her new day. Each day, she would rush to her phone to see his cheerful message with a big red heart he used as a signature. But the "Ping" that sounded this Saturday morning at 7:00 a.m. — following their disastrous dinner the night before — was not from Michael. It was from her boss, Hal, a real tool bag.

"You going to be at work Sunday?" the text said in his usual shorthand.

She returned the phone to the nightstand, rolled over, and went back to sleep.

The clock on the kitchen wall read 10:15 as she poured a cup of coffee. She returned the carton of Half & Half to the refrigerator, but before closing it, she removed two magnets fastening photos to the door — her "family wall," as she called it — where she kept her most prized pictures. She studied the two photos: one of Michael hugging her in front of a sunset on a beach in Anguilla; the other of the two of them crossing the finish line together in a Brooklyn half-marathon, arms raised in triumph.

She studied the photos for a long moment and felt a pang like a physical blow to her stomach. It was a combination of the fear of losing Michael and the apprehension of possibly making a mistake by marrying him. She put the two magnets together, positive pole to negative pole. The magnets clicked into place solidly. Next, she turned one pole around and tried to get them to click. They repelled each other, just as she and Michael had been doing too frequently of late. The content of their argument the night before might have seemed small to anyone listening, but what if life with him were to become a constant series of rebuffs like that?

She chided herself for thinking she'd had it all figured out, when now, she realized she had nothing figured out. She returned the photos to the refrigerator "wall," face down.

Her mother's wedding veil sat in a plastic bag on the dining-room table. She stepped into the dining room to grab the bag, then headed to the stairs leading to the attic. She needed to put the veil back in its heirloom case now that she had decided — after tossing and turning all night — to put their wedding on hold. Before ascending the stairs, though, she called the realtor working with them on a condo purchase. The condo was to be their new home. She and Michael had planned to buy the place in two weeks, a month before the wedding.

"On hold? Is there a problem, dear?" the realtor asked, her tone concerned.

"I need time to work something out."

"How much time?"

"I don't know yet, but I'll get back to you with details."

She needed time to ponder her relationship with Michael. He had used the word "deceive," which insinuated he did not trust her. If that was true, then what was the point of getting married? The foundation of any relationship had to be trust. Waiting before signing a thirty-year mortgage was small change when weighed against signing on for thirty, forty, fifty years, or more, in a marriage to someone who didn't trust you.

She felt the pang again as she climbed the stairs, her legs heavy from carrying the weight of a world that had suddenly come crashing down on her.

When she reached the attic, she went to the section where her parents' things were stored. It had been two years since her mom passed away. Six weeks after that, her dad suffered a massive stroke. Her parents had been living in Washington state at the time, and after his stroke, she had moved her dad back east so he could be close to her. She found a high-quality nursing home in Norwalk, Connecticut, within an hour's drive from Garden City on Long Island — where she lived — which allowed her to visit him regularly.

After placing her dad in the nursing home, she had flown to Washington to clean out her parents' house in Mt. Vernon, seventy miles north of Seattle. She got rid of most of their things, selling the furniture and donating clothes to Goodwill, before putting the house on the market to pay for the nursing home. But she did keep several boxes, not just the wedding veil, but boxes of old photos and one old suitcase that had special meaning for her dad. She was happy to save the items since they offered a time capsule on her parents' life together, and her life as their daughter.

What a happy childhood it had been.

Her parents had been deeply in love, a love that had enveloped her as well, though she didn't think too much about how lucky she had been to grow up in a house filled with such warmth. Like most children who grow up cherished by their parents, she had taken her parents love for each other for granted, like breathing good, fresh air.

Now, she ran her fingers along the gossamer fabric of the veil, which had yellowed a bit with age but was still stunningly beautiful. Her grandmother, who had come from Ireland as a small girl, had knit the wedding veil for her daughter, Peggy's mom, and Peggy had planned to wear it to honor the family tradition. After returning the veil to its heirloom case, she set the box atop another one that had "Save — Special Photos" written in magic marker in her mom's fine, delicate hand. Overtaken by a sudden impulse to explore the contents inside, she pulled up a chair. She opened the box, eager to reconnect with her mom and family memories.

Immersing herself in fond memories from her childhood would serve as a tonic to the overwhelming sadness she felt at the moment in terms of Michael.

She took a handful of the photos from the top of the box and filtered through them, smiling as she studied one after another like reading cards. She paused to look at one from her sixth birthday party, an outing to a local skating rink.

The photo showed her mom cutting the birthday cake with precision, as a sea of young girls' faces squeezed in close. Peggy recalled having tried to wrestle the knife from her mom to do the cutting herself only to have her mom say, curtly, "I make the rules, Peggy!" It was a terse rebuke intended to show Peggy who was boss in their mother/daughter relationship. Her friends loved her mom for how kind she was to them, but they had a nickname for her, "Joani-saurus Rex," for how tough she could be. Her mom had standards certainly, or as she would tell Peggy, often in front of her friends, "I make the rules, honey, until you're old enough. Then I'll turn the keys over to you, and the driving will be your job, but both of us will know I did my best to put you on the right road in life."

Her mom had a fun side, and Peggy had many special memories of the time spent with her mom, including singing in the car. They had a deal that when they pulled into a parking place, her mom would not turn the engine off until the song on the radio was over. So many times, they had sat in the grocery store lot with the car idling, and together they sang with Cindi Lauper, "Oh, girls just wanna have fuuuuuuun!"

Next, she came across a few of her family having fun together.

She found one of her at age seven in front of a beach pizza place. They were living in Boston then.

Every Sunday during the summer, they would go to the beach, and they would always choose some restaurant where they could have dinner before heading home. She liked the beach pizza place they had found on this particular Sunday, since it had cool fishing nets hanging from the ceiling and surfboards tacked to the walls. But her dad had turned to her mom and said, "Dicey crowd. Let's try another place. Everyone here looks like they burned out in the sixties." Seven-year-old Peggy wasn't buying it. "Hey, guys, I didn't burn out in the sixties," she said, as her dad snapped a photo of her wearing a long, dark pout.

Toward the bottom of the box were photos of her parents, Declan and Joan, together as a couple. Running was their "thing." Each morning, they'd be up at 5:30, lace up their Nikes, and be out the door for a six-mile training run before starting the day. She found photos of them giving thumbs-up as they ran along First Avenue together in the NYC

Marathon, hugging as they crossed the finish line together, always together, running stride for stride.

Then, just after Peggy started college, her mom got sick, and that changed everything. Peggy was reminded of this when she came across an anthology called *The Four Million*, with "The Gift of the Magi" by O. Henry as the first story.

O. Henry had written the story for a magazine in 1905, depicting the selflessness of a young couple who searched for the perfect Christmas gifts for each other. Peggy had found a book with the story, an original edition of a 1935 printing, in a rare-books store and had given it to them as a Christmas present one year in recognition of their love for O. Henry.

The story of "The Gift of the Magi" had always been their "beacon," as her parents called it — which they characterized as "one plus one equals one." They had formed a principle around the story — the Gift of the Magi Principle — which expressed their idea that when two people get married, they become one, and the "marriage journey" is to continually find ways to support each other.

That was never truer than after her mom got sick.

Her mom had no symptoms when diagnosed with lung cancer in her early fifties. It came as a shock, not only because her mom was a non-smoker and ate broccoli "up the wazoo," as she said it, but she had just set an age-group record in a 15K. Doctors thought they had caught it early, but a year later, it came back. This time, in her other lung, and a year after that, it came back in her bones. She fought it for four years before she passed away.

As Peggy placed the book back in the box, she spotted her mom's suitcase in a corner, the one she'd had shipped east with the photos. The suitcase had a special meaning for her dad, but it was still too raw an issue for her.

The suitcase contained her mom's clothes that her dad had packed. It had been time for her mom's next treatment, which meant driving from their home in Mt. Vernon to Seattle. Her mom liked to stay at a hotel in the city after receiving treatments at Swedish Hospital in Seattle. The hotel represented a small break from the tedium of returning home immediately after her hospital stay to lie in bed. That was the remarkable thing about her mom, her unflagging optimism along with her courage. She never considered herself a victim. "People get stuff," she often said. "Me, I got lung cancer. But I do like the spinach omelet I get from room service at the Hotel Vintage."

They had been about to leave for Seattle when the doctor called. He told them it would not be wise to come. Her mom's latest tests indicated that the cancer had spread to several organs, and the doctor did not need to explain the negative impact of a car trip. It was shortly after that, less than a week later, that her mom passed away at home. Her dad had saved the suitcase, filled with her clothes for what would have been their last trip together.

The phone rang downstairs, and Peggy snapped out of her reverie to answer it, but by the time she got to the kitchen, the ringing had stopped.

She wished she hadn't run so fast, since the message was from her boss, Hal, a follow up to the text he had sent that morning.

"You going to be at work tomorrow? See you then."

Such a zero! He knew that she and Michael used their weekends to do wedding errands. But now that she had decided to delay the wedding, no way would she tell that to Hal. She was the top performer in the office, valued by the CEO. Let Hal think she was busy on Sunday.

She went back upstairs to look at more photos, but she couldn't find any additional pictures of her with her mom and dad. She did find several photos of her alone with her mom. In the photos, she was an infant in her mom's arms.

Where's dad? she wondered. As she sorted through

the photos, she came upon a note from her aunt Eileen to her mom. Her mom was very close to her sister. "How are you doing?" Eileen wrote in the note. "How are you holding up since the separation?"

Separation?

Peggy leaned back in her chair. What separation?

Had there been a time when her parents' idyllic love story had not been so idyllic? Had there been a time when her mom and dad had parted ways?

Separation? How could that be?

She closed the box and stared at the blank wall, in shock.

Chapter Three

Peggy received a text from her Aunt Eileen the next day, Sunday.

"I saw you were trying to call me yesterday. Peter and I just got back from Spain last night. What can I do for you, honey?" the text read.

Her aunt had lived on the Upper East Side in Manhattan when Peggy was small. She would take Peggy to the intersection of 68th Street and First Ave to stand on the corner at the eighteen-mile mark to cheer for her parents as they went by in the New York City Marathon each year. Aunt Eileen and Uncle Peter had no children, and Peggy felt a special bond with them. Since they had retired, they often traveled the world and from her aunt's text, Spain had been their latest destination.

"Can I see you?" Peggy texted back.

"When?"

"Today?"

"You know where we live."

Her aunt lived in Cutchogue, on the north fork of Long Island about an hour and a half drive from Garden City. Traffic was light that Sunday afternoon, and Peggy made good time. Eileen welcomed her into the living room of her tidy, white Craftsman house that overlooked Long Island Sound.

"Uncle Peter is running errands, but sit and tell me what I can do for you, love."

Peggy told Eileen about the note she had found in the box in the attic, and Eileen's face took on a pensive cast.

"Ah, yes, that was a time when your mom suffered from post-partum depression after you were born. She had a bad case of it. Her anxieties continued beyond their first anniversary, but your dad couldn't see it, or refused to. Their honeymoon period crashed down hard as a result."

"Why did they split?"

"Your dad was making a strong mark as a college administrator even as a young guy. He devised a concept for an innovative school to teach at-risk kids, and an investor, an 'angel,' offered to bankroll him. But it meant your dad would have to leave his good-paying job at the university, and your mom balked.

"Really? That's not like her."

"I know, but it was then. She told him, 'You're putting us at risk, just as I have brought a new life into the world?' He said he'd be in a better position to support the family if he could follow his dream. 'But what if you fail?' she said. 'You won't have a job.' The investor was offering half a million dollars and he had to grab it or lose it, he said. Still, your mom refused to bend — biology had her in its grip — and she told your dad he had to choose. His career, or her. Your dad got very upset at being backed into a corner, and their disagreement turned to rancor. Then bitterness. Ultimately, he passed on the opportunity with the investor, but he moved out to show his displeasure.

"I never knew," she said, though she could see her and Michael's intransigence mirrored in their story.

"You were a honeymoon baby, and you were too young to know."

"How long did their separation last?"

"Six months, but they found a way to patch it up. Hard feelings could have broken them apart for good, but they found a way to repair the damage."

"How?"

"It was about the time of their second anniversary and your dad came to your mom. She was in her car in the driveway about to back up, and your dad pulled in behind her. They met bumper to bumper. As they each got out of their cars, they stood face to face. 'I can't live without you,' your dad said, and your mom said, 'Separation from you has been agony.' He told her, 'I'm sorry I was oblivious to what you were feeling.' And she said, 'I'm sorry I did not support you.' In that instant, they resolved to repair their relationship. 'Build on what you've built,' was a term they coined from their experience."

"'Build on what you've built.' What does that mean?"

"Rather than throw everything away when conflict arises, look at the value of what you've created together, the shared experiences, and build on that. It was a concept they developed from 'The Gift of the Magi' story."

"They loved that story. One Christmas, I gave them a first-edition of the book."

"In the story, as you know, each person gives up what is most valuable to them so they can offer a gift of great value to the other. The husband and wife each act selflessly, but the part that struck your mom and dad so powerfully is how the couple gave to each other without prompting or hesitation, and did it simultaneously."

Peggy sat on the sofa, looking out to the sea, thinking of Michael and all the memories they had created.

"Your parents added a quality of forgiveness to what they called the Gift of the Magi Principle. The idea that if someone hurts us, as your parents hurt each other, it's critical to put bitterness aside. We can hold on to our anger — on some level there's satisfaction — but that does us no good. In the end, when we refuse to let go of our resentment, it costs us more than it costs the other person, because holding onto bitterness cuts us off from our life source."

Peggy conjured an image of the hose getting pinched.

"I get it," she said.

"Your parents saw the folly in letting ego dominate. Both had hurt each other, but they chose to put their pride aside. That's why they created an Anniversary Box."

"Anniversary Box? What's that?"

"As I said, their second anniversary was coming up, so your mom and dad decided to establish a routine. Each year, to mark their marriage, they would identify something that made their relationship strong. They would write it down and put the message into the Anniversary Box."

"Tell me."

"They wrote two messages, one to capture what they had missed on their first anniversary and a second one to start a tradition. Each anniversary thereafter they would compose a message of support for each other to affirm their union — one plus one equals one — then add a new message to build on that foundation for the year ahead. That way over time, they created a pathway to enduring love that was tangible, unbreakable, and sprang from an event that could have torn them apart, but now made them stronger. Ultimately, your dad got another chance to start his own company, and when that happened, your mom supported him fully. He supported her to become a painter, which was her dream. The concept worked."

"Where is this Anniversary Box?"

"Your mom told me she kept it in her art room with her valuables. I have a painting of it." Eileen said, and she went into her bedroom.

When she returned, she carried a painting of a finely crafted wooden box. "Joan gave this to Peter and me, and it hangs over our bed. She was quite an artist, your mom. She got that talent from our dad. He was a fireman by day, but he'd moonlight at night as a sign painter."

Eileen handed the painting to Peggy. It showed the polished wooden box with a rose on the front and the phrase "One plus one equals one."

"My mom loved roses," Peggy said.

"She put a rose on the box as a symbol for love, but

she wanted the stories inside to sustain the rose so it would never lose its bloom."

Never lose its bloom. The phrase resonated with Peggy, and she took a picture with her phone, then said, "How do I find the box?"

"I don't know. Your dad would know, but in his state, he can't speak, obviously."

She outlined the rose with her finger as the two sat in silence and Peggy watched the sun set on the water, thinking.

"I should go," she said.

It was dark by the time she got home, but she went straight to the attic to find the O. Henry anthology she had given her parents as a Christmas gift.

She wanted to reread the story that had prompted her parents to strengthen their love and create an Anniversary Box to mark that. She found the box that read "Save – Special Photos," and she sorted through the pictures until she found the O. Henry book. Then under the dim light of a single bulb in the attic, she reread "The Gift of the Magi."

Yes, she thought after finishing the story. The husband, Jim, and wife, Delia, give selflessly to each other. Jim bought a set of combs for Delia's beautiful, long hair, and she bought Jim a chain for his beloved watch. But she sold her hair to buy the chain, and he sold his watch to buy her the combs. Their gestures — to give to each other simultaneously — made the act of giving more valuable than the gifts themselves.

She leaned back in her chair and pondered the image of her parents standing together in the driveway, poised to give each other the gift of forgiveness and set themselves on a life-long journey to create an enduring love.

Her parents had been married for twenty-four years — nearly twenty-five — which meant that the Anniversary Box contained twenty-four entries with inspirational messages. Those messages could offer her a guide to repair her relationship with Michael and set it on a similar pathway to last a lifetime.

She went to close the book, but she noticed a small bulge at the back. She flipped to the back cover and found a key taped under the flap.

She removed the tape and fingered the key.

Was this the key to the Anniversary Box?

Could this be the key to her parents' treasure chest of twenty-four profound statements? If only she could find the box, she'd be able to unlock the secret to love and know how to make it last forever.

She weighed the key in her hand, pondering a strategy.

She had to find that box!

Chapter Four

Hal was careful not to harass her in an overt way, nothing that would get him hauled in front of a #MeToo jury.

But he had a special talent for pushing her buttons.

"Good Monday morning," he said, accenting the "Monday" as she walked into the office with a Starbucks in one hand and her satchel of take-home assignments in the other. She smiled in his direction, but he turned away so he wouldn't have to acknowledge her attempt at civility.

Peggy had come to New York from Washington state after college. During college, she had taken a summer internship at NBC, where she had performed well in the social-media division. One day while in the city, a girlfriend from Soul Cycling suggested she apply to the company where she worked. "Great future," the friend said, describing opportunities at a tech start-up in Silicon Alley, the neighborhood in New York between 14th and 23rd Streets, where new tech companies blossomed daily.

When Peggy got back to school, she sent in her resume, and the CEO invited her to New York for an interview. He loved her passion and hired her upon graduation. She chose to live in Garden City on Long Island because she could rent a two-story condo with an attic and get it cheaper than renting a one-bedroom in Manhattan. Within a year after she started at the tech company, the firm opened an office in Mineola, the town next to Garden City, and she requested a transfer to the new operation to save on the commute. The job was great, but the decision to switch offices from Manhattan to Mineola had two liabilities. The first being that Michael lived in

Brooklyn, and that meant they saw less of each other at a point when they were getting serious. They dealt with that by planning to get married. But the second — and worse — liability was that she had to report to Hal, who oversaw the operation in Mineola.

Hal took special delight in making her life miserable.

Mid-thirties, he was one of the founders of the start-up. Swizzle-stick-thin, he sported a man bun and a manicured goatee, which she had once observed him trimming at his desk with a tiny scissors and hand-held mirror. She described him to friends as "Immaculate dress, poor follow through," which is why, she surmised, he put so much pressure on those who reported to him to perform at an extra-high level. He needed to pull the wool over the eyes of the CEO back in the city to cover his incompetence.

"Hal's mad you didn't come into work yesterday," said Gail, her co-worker, as they huddled near the watercooler that afternoon.

"Sunday is a day of rest. He doesn't know that?"

"He's under pressure to show growth to his colleagues in the city."

"But why is he such a pain in the ass to me?"

"He likes you, Peggy."

"Likes me?"

"Yeah, he flirted with you when you started with us and you blew him off. That hurt his feelings."

"What feelings?"

"I'm thinking he wants you to go out with him. He knows you and Michael have been having challenges, which is how I heard him refer to the dust-ups you and Michael have been having lately. Ask me, and I'd say he's hoping to weasel his way in."

"He can wait till hell freezes over."

"He's set to rake in a ton on stock options once the company goes public, Peggy."

"Yecchhh!"

"Where are you going?" Gail asked as Peggy

checked her watch and reached for her coat.

"This is Monday, the day I get to see my father. It's in my contract."

She had put a clause in her contract with the CEO — trading time off to see her dad for less pay — so she could leave early on Mondays and Thursdays to drive to Norwalk, Connecticut, to visit her father in his nursing home. She tried to see her dad at least once on weekends as well, when not consumed with wedding plans.

Her dad's stroke — coming just six weeks after her mom passed away — occurred in his brain stem. This was especially serious because a stroke in that area can affect both sides of the body and create what doctors call a "locked-in" state. Patients lose their ability to speak and movements below the neck are impaired.

"Your dad's situation has aspects of 'locked-in,'" the doctors told her. "We can't know for sure the extent of the damage. Therefore, the more you can talk to him, even though it won't be certain he's hearing you, can be therapeutic. So, just giving him a chance to see you and listen to you is the strongest medicine we can offer him at this point."

Her real goal was to get her dad into a trial that could address (and hopefully cure) those aspects of "locked-in," which combined aphasia — an inability to hear and comprehend words — with a lack of mobility in the limbs. Her hope was that the drug used in the trial could repair his brain stem and eliminate the anguish he might be experiencing being trapped inside a body that no longer worked. That's what kept her up at night; her concern for her dad that, after a lifetime as a top runner with a toned body, he could be experiencing such anguish. He had done so much for her mom, and given so much, it pained Peggy to see him imprisoned by the stroke. But the drug, though promising, was costly at $10,000 per month. So she continued to write countless letters to petition the two pharma companies that offered drugs that could be used in the trial. She hoped to gain acceptance into their philanthropic programs and get the fee waived. But to date, no luck.

She stopped at a Barnes & Noble after she got off the highway in Norwalk to buy a Scrabble game. The game was a new idea she had come up with. Since the doctor encouraged her to talk to her dad, she decided to try to make it fun.

She hugged her dad as she entered his room and pulled up a chair beside his bed.

"Hello, Dad. We're going to talk family history today, okay?" she said as she signaled to the nurse that she was set to go and could take it from there. Her dad stared at her, not looking at her directly, more just gazing vacantly in her direction.

"You met Mom at a dance in Boston, remember?

You were both teaching school after college. You had come from New York, and she had graduated from a small women's college in Boston. You remember that night, right? The dance was at Alumni Hall at her old school, and you heard about the dance from a friend. All the guys wore suits, but you showed up in a shirt with a hand-embroidered sun on the back. You were out of step, Dad, not the first time in your life, but mom spotted you across the room with that big, bright sun on your back, a true target, and she asked you to dance.

"I don't know if you can hear me, or if you understand what I'm saying, but the doctor said it's good if I try to jog your memory. So I came up with a new idea this visit. I'm going to play a game of Scrabble with you. You always loved this game, remember?"

She opened the Scrabble box and spread the board out across his lap as he lay in bed. She used the little wooden tiles with letters on them to spell out the word "wise."

"You were a wise counselor to me when I was growing up, Dad. When I was seventeen and wanted a car so I could drive to school instead of taking the bus, you let me have one. But you said there was one rule: use your head, you told me. I loved the way you put responsibility onto me."

She focused on her dad's eyes, so soft and plaintive, but his gaze continued to sail past her to a spot on the wall.

She selected the tiles to spell "shortstop."

"I had so many great times with you, Dad. You would hit balls to me in the street after dinner as I pretended to be a shortstop. You always wanted to be a shortstop. You went out for track in high school to get in shape for baseball, but you came in third in a freshman cross-country meet, and after that, the coach wouldn't let you leave the track team. It was great you became a runner because you introduced Mom to the sport, and that became a source of great joy for the two of you.

"Mom was a special girl, wasn't she, Dad?" She spelled out "special," then "mom."

"Mom and I spent a lot of time in the car when I was growing up. She drove me to track meets in junior high — and we talked. She told me how she admired you for your independence. I know there were times she called you pig-headed, and truth is, you are, Dad. You've always been the guy with the handcrafted sun on your shirt while the other guys wore suits. But Mom had her own mind, too, and the two of you had a special bond. Two peas in a pod."

She spelled out "peas in a pod."

"Mom told me how much she loved her dad — as much as I love you. When Mom was a little girl in Boston, her dad would take her for walks around Castle Island. He'd buy her a PayDay candy bar, and they'd watch the ships sail out to sea. Her dad was a Boston fireman. Other girls had fathers who worked in office buildings, but Mom was proud that her dad was a Boston fireman."

She spelled "fireman."

"Her dad grew up in a rough and tumble South Boston neighborhood. As a kid, he and his friends made money pinching ice off the back of ice trucks, then they'd run ahead to the row houses in front of the truck to sell the ice at a discount. He enlisted in the Navy at sixteen by lying about his age and spent three years fighting the Japanese in the Pacific. When Mom was a little girl, her father would often take her to the firehouse with him. The firehouse had guys like Bucko Bastinelli who walked around with a copy of *Life Magazine* in his back pocket. That's also where Bucko kept his cash for the bookie operation he ran. That's why you married Mom, isn't it, Dad? You wanted a girl who learned about the world from a front-row seat in the firehouse at Scolley Square."

She spelled the word "kick."

"Mom had kick. After college, she rented an apartment in Boston with three classmates.

Cockroaches swarmed the place, and they brought the landlord to court to get their money back. The slumlord's lawyer put the four girls on the stand. The first three babbled on about how bugs scared them. Then the lawyer put Mom on the stand. He called her a 'prissy little thing.' She was perfectly put together with her scarf always tied just right, and he said, 'You probably never saw a cockroach in your privileged life.' She asked the judge for a pen and paper, and drew a picture of a cockroach that would have made the cover of *Biology Magazine*. Then she said to the lawyer, looking him straight in the eye, 'You mean like this?' Her sketch convinced the judge, and they won the case. She had kick, all right."

Peggy closed the Scrabble board and leaned in close to her father.

"Here's why I'm telling you all this, Dad. You and Mom created an atmosphere of love for me when I was growing up, and I'm so grateful. I know you're here because of all you gave Mom while she was sick.

The a-fib you developed from the stress, and the blood clots that followed. Doctors told me it was the stress of Mom's illness that enlarged your heart and led to your stroke. You were trying to run your business and be a 24/7 caregiver during those four years Mom was sick. You carried all that on your shoulders.

"You loved Mom, Dad, and I know she loved you, but I learned that you and Mom also had a rough time in the beginning of your marriage. I saw the letter Aunt Eileen sent Mom, asking her how she was holding up during the separation."

Her dad continued to stare at Peggy in a vague way, but still, she didn't know if he was seeing her or hearing her.

"I never knew that you and Mom had turbulence, and I hope you don't mind, but I need to talk about this."

She took a deep breath.

"You see, I'm having a tough time with Michael at the moment. We're different from each other, and that has always been the attraction. I love Michael for how different we are, but I fear our relationship is breaking apart. Being different brought us together, but now it's feeling corrosive. It's destroying us, but I really don't want to live without him.

"I need to know what you and Mom did to fix things, what you did to set yourself on a powerful course after nearly breaking apart.

"Aunt Eileen told me about the Anniversary Box you and Mom created. I'm thinking that Anniversary Box could unlock the secret. I'm thinking the stories you and Mom wrote to each other might give me a pathway to create a life with Michael where our love, which is suffering at the moment, can be strong and last forever. You and Mom didn't just patch things up, you created a towering love for the ages. I need to know how you did it.

"I'm sorry to put all this on you, Dad. They tell me you can't understand any of what I'm saying anyway. I see you looking at me, but I don't know if you're comprehending. I hope you're not, actually, because I'm embarrassed to be talking like this. I could have seen it growing up, how you and mom created your special bond, but I missed it. Now I want to know. I need to know how you did it."

She paused.

"Action has always been your thing, Dad. Oh, I so wish I was little again so you could give me your wise advice."

A nurse stepped into the room. "He's getting tired, dear. He fatigues easily, as you know."

"Yes, you're right. I should let him rest."

"That would be a good idea. It's so good of you to come here as often as you do."

"Yes," Peggy said, and she packed the Scrabble game and put it on a shelf beside his bed. But before she left, she took a handful of letter tiles she had held back and spelled out one more message across his lap: "I love you, Dad."

Chapter Five

*P**ing!*
This time the ping was from Michael. The message was short, though it did come with a heart icon, a good sign. "I need to go to San Francisco on a three-day project with a bank client. Can I see you when I get back?"

Her fingers hovered over the keys on her phone as she pondered how best to express the stomach-turned-upside-down confusion she was feeling, when the doorbell rang.

It was a delivery man with a package from Michael.

She opened the box and inside was a Titleist 2 golf ball with a note. "Can I take a shot to get us out of the rough? I promise not to shank it this time."

Ah, he was drawing on his love of golf, a game that consumed him. His biggest dream in life was to play a round of golf with Phil Mickelson. When he was a boy, Michael and his dad would watch golf on TV together. Phil Mickelson was his dad's idol, and Michael, who lost his dad in a car accident when he was just ten-years-old, adopted Phil Mickelson as his idol.

She called him, but his phone had been forwarded to his assistant, who said Michael was on his way to San Francisco. "I assume he's in the air already since he forwarded his phone. Would you like to leave a message?"

"Tell him, yes on the golf ball. He'll know what that means."

She couldn't help but smile as she bounced the ball in her palm, and for the first time in days, she felt light again. She couldn't wait to tell him about the Anniversary Box and the promise of what that offered to get them out of the "rough."

What makes love blossom? And with the bloom of the rose so delicate, how do we keep the bloom alive?

Peggy looked to connect with her mom's friends to learn that answer. She hoped they could recall things her mom had talked about that belied passions that could offer guidance.

Most of her mom's friends lived in Washington state, where Peggy's family had lived since moving from Boston when Peggy was in grade school. Other than a four-year stint in California at Santa Clara University before moving to New York, she had lived in Washington. Thus, she knew many of her mom's friends.

Her mom had earned a formidable reputation as a painter in the Northwest and had an eclectic group of friends, including fellow painters, crafts people, flower arrangers, hard-core athletes she would train with for marathons, musicians, and assorted activists — really anybody with an open mind, which appealed to her mom's egalitarian instincts. Peggy found email addresses for many of them and sent out a blast asking her mom's friends if she could contact them.

All responded with open arms.

Peggy connected first with Tricia, who owned a flower shop in Mt. Vernon.

"Your mom and dad loved their beer and pizza nights," Tricia said, as she spoke on the phone. "'Coors beer and pizza,' they called it. I don't know why your mom always called it 'Coors beer and pizza.' I guess she just liked that brand of beer. But that was her code name for 'conversation.' If ever you asked her about the pizza, what kind she liked, she'd pinch two fingers together, leaving a narrow gap, and say, 'Food is that much of it.' What she really loved was the chance to go out with your dad and have conversation."

Peggy concurred. She had loved going out to pizza places with her parents when she was growing up, since they always included her in the conversation. "But by the time I was a teenager, I couldn't wait for Friday night basketball games so I could get out of hanging with the Ps," she said.

Tricia laughed, "Well, they carried on that tradition after you moved away. I only wish I had owned stock in Coors."

Then Peggy caught up with Brandi, a spinning instructor at her mom's health club.

"'Build on what you've built.' I learned that from your mom," Brandi said.

"Did you ever hear her talk about an Anniversary Box?"

"I did. In fact, my husband, Carl, and I started our own Anniversary Box because of your mom. There was a time I almost threw Carl out of the house after he had a fling with a red-head from the Wild

Buffalo. But instead—at your mom's suggestion—we saw a counselor, and this year, our girl finished college and our boy graduated high school.

"'Build on what you've built,'" Brandi repeated. "I will always be grateful to your mom for her support when I was at my lowest."

Another friend, Stella, owned a gallery in Seattle. She often showed Peggy's mom's paintings, and the money her mom made contributed to the family's income.

"This is a long-winded story, but it has a point," Stella said when Peggy reached out to her.

"One day, a lady knocked on your mom's door and asked if she could clean her house. The lady was from Mexico and had a green card. She was starting a business and looking for customers. Your mom said yes and became fast friends with the lady. Your mom would host birthday parties for the lady's kids, because she lived in a small apartment with her husband who worked as a sheet-rock laborer, and they didn't have room at their home for parties.

"One day the lady told your mom that her six-year-old daughter had developed severe stomach cramps. The lady didn't have health insurance, so she took the little girl to the emergency room where they billed her $2500 for a CT scan. Fortunately, the little girl was okay, but now the lady had the bill, and the hospital assigned her case to a collection agency when she couldn't afford to pay it. You following me so far?" Stella said.

"Yes."

"Well, your mom showed up at my gallery in Seattle and asked how much the painting she had brought in a week earlier might fetch. It was a gorgeous painting of a Skagit County sunset. I told her if we showcased it for a month, it might bring $7,500. She asked how much if we sold it right away, and I told her I could get $1900.

"Your mom and dad had a thing. He'd go to the casinos when he had a consulting job in the

Caribbean, and he'd take his winnings and convert them into $100 bills. Instead of buying your mom Clarins Body Cream at the airport duty-free shop on the way home, he'd give her the $100 bills for good luck. She had six of those $100 bills in her purse the day she came to see me. I gave her a check to cover the $1900 I knew the painting could fetch, and she put that together with the $600 in her purse and gave it to the cleaning lady to cover the $2500 hospital bill."

"Cool story," Peggy said.

"That story made it into the Anniversary Box under a heading, 'Be uncommonly kind.' That was a resolution your mom and dad made that if one of them saw a need to help someone, the other would offer support without question. Often couples fight if one person wants to spend family money unilaterally, but your mom and dad looked at it differently. They believed in the idea that all people are connected, and it was the job of a married couple to see themselves as part of that greater connection, and so they always trusted each other's judgment."

Tad, the owner of the pizza place, knew her parents well, of course. And he was only too happy to help Peggy solve her puzzle.

"'Right a wrong'," he said. "I remember that one."

A former hippie turned buttoned-down professional, he described how he would sit with them when they visited his pizza restaurant and the crowd had thinned out. He'd pull up a chair and join their conversation. He spoke of one evening when he'd shared a story with them about a disagreement he was having with his kitchen crew. That led to a discussion about disagreements in general.

"If they had a disagreement, they told me they would not take it to bed with them. They would always talk it out, no matter how long it took. To them, saying sorry was not a crime; saying sorry was a sign of strength."

Not bad advice.

"'Not me. We'," said Donna, one of her mom's walking friends.

Donna was a state senator, the first African-American elected to the Senate from Skagit County. Donna had been a member of her mom's running group until she injured her back in a car accident. After she took up walking to keep fit, Peggy's mom, who had designed the graphics for her campaign, walked with Donna to keep her company.

"I think of this as their Hood River story," Donna said. "Your mom had been invited to an art show in Hood River, Oregon, an event all the big art buyers in the Northwest were scheduled to attend. It would have advanced her career. But the fee was huge—something like $6,000—and she didn't have that amount. Your dad had a client who wanted him to attend a conference that same weekend where the man planned to introduce your dad to major educational leaders who could help him build his company. The only catch was that your dad had to bring his spouse, because that was the theme of the conference. Your dad had an alternative offer to speak at a competing conference where they promised to pay him $6,000. He took the second invitation so he could pay for your mom's Hood River conference, but she turned down the Hood River invitation so she could attend your dad's spouse event."

Peggy nodded. "Yup, sounds like them."

"How's that for a top-shelf 'Gift of the Magi' story?" said Donna.

Peggy hung up with Donna, but she couldn't help but marvel at how powerful it could be to have an Anniversary Box to make things good again.

Chapter Six

As Peggy stood at the stove steaming kale to make dinner for herself, Michael called. "I'm still in San Francisco. But I get back tomorrow afternoon. Did you get the golf ball?"

"Yes, but I thought you might have asked Phil Mickelson to sign it."

"Very funny. Will you let me take a shot to see if I can get us close to the pin?"

"Phil Mickelson writes all your lines?"

"Don't mock me. Someday, my dream will come true and I'll play with Phil."

"I'm sure you will. Yes, I want to see you, too, Michael. I can't wait to tell you about the

Anniversary Box."

"What's that?"

"It's based on 'build on what you've built.'"

"What are you talking about?"

"I've learned so much in the past few days, and I'm eager to share it all with you."

"I have a meeting in Garden City when I get back tomorrow. Our firm just signed the Village of Garden City as a client, and I asked to meet with the fire chief. They tell me he's the club champ with contacts in the golf world. Maybe he can help me get an invitation to play a round with Phil Mickelson."

"I don't know about golf, but my grandfather was a fireman."

"I doubt they have Bucko Bastinelli on staff. And I doubt they have bookies who carry cash inside the pages of *Life Magazine* in their back pockets."

"How boring."

"My meeting with the fire chief should be over by six tomorrow. The firehouse is around the corner from your apartment. Will you meet me when you get off work? I'll take you to dinner at Prost afterwards."

"Do I need to bring the golf ball?"

"I won't need a prompt. I'm going to show the whole world how much I love you — you'll see."

While eating lunch at her desk the next day — and checking her watch every two seconds, hoping to make six o'clock come sooner — Peggy got a call from Donna, the state senator from Washington. Donna had a contact at a pharma company she wanted to share.

"When we spoke this week, I had asked you how your dad was doing, and you told me about the trial you were hoping to get him into for his stroke, remember?"

"Of course."

"Well, a lobbyist stopped by my office this morning. His name is Doug Phillips. He mentioned that one of the two drug companies that makes that drug with such promise just opened an office in Seattle. I told him about all the letters you had written to the philanthropic programs, and Doug said he'd be happy to help. Email me a sample of the letter you've been sending to the companies, and I'll share it with him and connect you two."

Donna gave Peggy a number to call to follow up with Doug Phillips, and Peggy thanked her profusely.

"Have you coordinated with sales yet?" Hal asked as he walked past her desk as she hung up with Donna.

His non-sequiturs did not surprise her, but this cryptic comment caught her off guard, since her job on the marketing side did not require her to initiate contact with the sales team. It was up to the sales team to contact her if they had a need.

"What?" she said, but she wanted to take it back as

soon as she said it because she could see the delight it gave him to confuse her.

"We need to expand productivity. I want marketing to play a greater role helping sales meet their numbers."

She recovered quickly. "Look, if the CEO needs to boost revenue, I'm happy to contribute. Ask sales to stop by my desk in the morning, and I'll be happy to help them."

Hal walked away with a vaunted air of superiority as if he had won a battle, and she called Doug Phillips.

"Yes, Donna told me about you," he said. "I'll take a look at the letter you've been sending the philanthropic guys. That drug is expensive, I know, so I'll do what I can to advocate for your dad."

"I can't tell you how grateful I am. Thank you, Mr. Phillips."

"No worries. I can't promise anything. But I'll see if I can find someone to help."

Not that staring at her watch had contributed, but finally six o'clock arrived. Others in the office had already started to put on coats. The work day ended at five o'clock, but everybody knew the quarter was ending soon, and nobody had a problem staying until six. But now that six o'clock had come, it was like a switch had been thrown.

"Where you going?" Hal asked her as he passed through the room, ignoring that others had already begun heading for the door.

"I'm going to see my f-i-a-n-c-é," she said, spelling out the word very slowly so he could choke on each letter.

At the firehouse, the doors to the bays that housed the city's two fire trucks were open. Inside, a group of firemen polished the engines, as Peggy found Michael waiting in the firehouse lobby. She spoke first to greet him.

"Welcome home," she said.

"I'm happy you're still talking to me."

"I've got lots I want to tell you."

She gestured to a sofa where they could sit. Michael listened intently as she told him about finding the letter from her aunt. She told him about the trouble her parents had experienced early in their relationship, and about learning those details from her aunt, including news that her parents had created an Anniversary Box to affirm their love for each other after resolving to repair their relationship. She showed him the photo on her phone she had taken of her aunt's painting of the Anniversary Box.

"Interesting concept."

"Each year, they would write a message to underscore their bond."

She told him about stories she had learned from her parents' friends, including "Right a Wrong," and "Be Uncommonly Kind," and "Not me. We."

"Can we find this Anniversary Box? We can use it as a guide."

"That's what I'm thinking."

"I like your plan."

"You're a good listener, Michael." She made two balled fists and clicked them together, like two magnets connecting. "I like it when we click."

"I don't like the pain of not clicking with you."

"Tell me, why do you like me?"

"You go first. Why do you like me enough to stick with me?"

"Remember when I ran the New York City Marathon? My parents used to run New York every year when I was a little girl, and I would stand on First Avenue with my Aunt Eileen and Uncle Peter and cheer them on. I wanted so badly to run that race after my mom passed away. You offered to run it with me to pace me. You helped me get through it, Michael, and only later did I learn that you had pulled your hamstring several days earlier and could barely walk. Yet you never mentioned your injury, and you ran beside me the whole way and never complained about your pain."

"I wanted to earn street cred with you."

"Well, you did, and that's why I don't want to lose you, despite the pain in the ass you can be. Deep down under that analytical coating, you're kind and thoughtful."

"You're putting a knock on us analysts? Without us, you poets wouldn't have wireless internet, ATM machines, or Tang."

"No knocks. I'm head over heels in love with you for the 'what adventure is next' spark you add to my life. You inspire me to be proactive and I love that."

"I have to confess, though. I do have a line in the sand, still."

"Oh, really? What line?"

"I can't get over the size of your student loans, Peggy. The fact that you never told me how big they were."

She stared at him, like hitting a wall.

"I told you, my mom was sick and I was helping

my dad. Do you really want to go back to square one on all this?"

"I have standards."

"You can't measure everything in life with a slide rule, Michael."

"You're not seeing my point of view."

"You'd throw it all away, throw us away? Over an intellectual construct?"

A long moment passed, and he didn't answer. That was answer enough for her.

"I'm sorry," she said. "I've got to go."

She walked to the door, pausing once to look back to see if he had moved. He had not moved, and with her hand on the doorknob she offered a parting word.

"Your pride, the thing that will be your undoing, Michael, is you never let emotion into any aspect of your life."

He didn't say anything, and after another long moment, she continued out the door.

She stepped to her car which she had parked on a patch of hard packed sand on the side of the firehouse. Her head was spinning as she sat behind the wheel and peered straight-ahead before turning the key in the ignition. She knew this was her own line in the sand — the final moment before she would start the car, pull away, and never look back.

She glanced to her right, to the Titleist 2 golf ball that sat on the passenger's seat. He had told her not to bring the golf ball, but on a hunch, she had brought it and had placed it on the seat. She took the ball in her hand, and squeezed it tight. It was warm from the early evening sun that poured through the window. She felt the warmth, and she made a decision. She opened the car door and turned to walk back across the hard packed sand to the firehouse, prepared to talk to him one more time. But she stopped when she saw Michael standing near the back bumper of her car. He had a sheepish grin on his face.

"We've done a lot of valuable things together," he

said. "Yes, it would be stupid to throw it all away."

"One of my mom and dad's friends, the guy who owns the pizza place in Washington, said my parents told him it was not a sign of weakness to say you're sorry. It's a sign of strength, they told him."

"I don't want to lose you over an intellectual construct."

She used her shoe to scratch a line in the sand between them.

"What are you doing?"

"I'm drawing a line in the sand," she said. When she finished etching the line with her right foot, she scratched it away with her left. "And now I'm erasing it. I don't like lines."

He gazed at her, with a puzzled look on his face.

She handed him the golf ball, then she stepped up close to him and looked into his eyes. "We've been rough on each other, Michael. I'm sorry for my part in that."

He took the golf ball and smiled. "I'm sorry for

using the word 'deceived' at dinner that night."

"Can we build on what we've built?"

"I'd like that."

"Can we find our way home again?"

"I have an idea," he said, as he punched keys on his phone.

"Who are you calling?"

"The fire chief. I'm sure he's still in his office."

"The fire chief? Why are you calling the fire chief?"

A moment later, the fire chief, a stout, craggy-faced man, appeared in the firehouse driveway in his full fire-chief regalia.

He had a look on his face as if he were fully aware of whatever it was Michael had cooked up.

"What's going on?" she said.

Michael stepped to the firehouse driveway. Peggy trailed behind him slowly, as the chief walked to one of the bays and took his place beside a fire truck.

"Chief, is this where I stand so you can recycle?"

Michael said as he stood above a drain in the driveway.

"What are you doing?" Peggy asked.

"We need to recycle this," Michael said, and he signaled to the chief who unwound the hose from the fire truck.

"Yeah, a little bit more to the left, get centered over the drain," the chief said, and Michael repositioned himself in the driveway.

"Okay, fire way, Chief," Michael said, and the look on Peggy's face was pure shock as a torrent of water erupted from the hose and doused Michael, who stood tall and stout in his suit and tie as he took the blow from a powerful hosing.

"Oh my God!" she said.

"See how much I love you? My love starts at one end of the hose and pours out the other," he said, trying to maintain his balance against the strong stream of water buffeting him.

"You set this up? You had me meet you at the firehouse so you could pull a stunt like this?"

"I analyzed how much water we'd need, and how much the chief can reclaim, and it all zeroes out — so no harm no fowl," he said, using his hands to slap back at the water.

"I want to feel I'm moving forward with my husband-to-be, Michael. Not moving backward, not static. Forward. Will you join me on the search for my parents' Anniversary Box?"

"You still plan to marry me? I heard you called the realtor to delay the closing on our new home," he said, as the chief turned off the hose.

"I'll call her back. I'll fix it. We can unlock my parent's secret together."

"I have an idea for the first entry in our own Anniversary Box," he said, shaking the water out of his ears.

He reach out to her, and she stepped gingerly toward him as water continued to stream off him and drip onto her brand-new shoes that had consumed nearly half her last paycheck.

"We'll call it 'Come in, the water's fine.'" He reached for her hand, and she let him take it.

"Are we good now?" he said.

"Yes, good," she said. She embraced him, laughing, as water dripped down his sleeves and out from under his pants and soaked her dress, and they rocked in each other's arms in the firehouse driveway.

"Remember canoodling in Idaho?"

"What are you talking about?"

"I like you because you let me get away with being Crazytown."

Chapter Seven

How do we make love grow? How do we nurture the rose so it will sustain its bloom and last forever?

The question compelled Peggy to accelerate her search for the Anniversary Box by expanding the outreach to her mom's friends. She hoped their stories might reveal details on her parents' secret for keeping love alive, especially help her gain insight into the wellspring that gave their love such depth — things a child can miss growing up because children are not yet wise enough to see.

She also hoped that someone might recall where in her mom's art room she had kept the Anniversary

Box among her valuables.

Next on her detective's list, she connected with Bernice, who owned a hand-crafted jewelry shop in downtown Mt. Vernon that doubled as her studio. Bernice had half red hair and half purple hair along with a series of shoulder tattoos visible on the Zoom call.

"I loved your mom, man," Bernice said, and she went straight to how impressed she was by the power of her mom's relationship with her dad. That's how Bernice expressed it, "I was blown away by how they resisted temptation."

"Temptation?"

"Your mom and dad were amazing, man. You didn't need to put a cop on their beat. Woody Allen once said, 'Only pigeons and Catholics mate for life,' but I'd add your mom and dad to that list."

"What do you mean?"

"Your mom was a famous artist in these parts. Put it this way, we have a few touchy-feely types who don't buy into Woody Allen's analogy."

"Carousers?"

"Let's just say we have guys who give hugs with a little extra *umph*. I remember art gallery openings in Seattle where your mom took more hits than a piñata at a Miami sweet-sixteen party. But your dad never let it bother him. He trusted her completely."

"I remember those Seattle openings. Squeezes fueled by wine."

"She trusted your dad, too. He was on the road a lot with his business. East coast, west coast, all around the globe. He worked with a lot of consultants and school officials. Some of them were very attractive, as I recall. But your mom never pressed him to explain."

"The phone rang a lot during dinnertime when I was growing up. My mom would answer it and pass the receiver to my dad, then go back to putting away groceries or whatever."

"They hit on something very important for couples, the idea of 'give each other gifts.'"

"What do you mean?"

"The world is full of ambiguity. The key is to live with that. You can't know everything going on in your spouse's life, so trust them to do the right thing. Give them that gift — of trust."

"That's quite a gift for one to give another."

Live with ambiguity. Peggy made a mental note to look for ways to apply that with Michael.

Give gifts to each other.

Another powerful lesson.

She closed out the video call with Bernice and smiled — she was learning important lessons, things she was sure had made their way into her parent's Anniversary Box that she could use as a guide to keep her own soon-to-be marriage on track.

Peggy was in the car on the way home from the grocery store that evening when she got a call from Kimberly, her "bestie" from Washington. They had been on the track team together during high school. "Friendly rivals," as Kimberly characterized it, with a friendship based on teasing honed during countless sleep-overs. In the 1500-meter race at the State Championship in their senior year, they had finished one/two. It was a photo finish, with an actual photo required to determine the winner, and it took the judges nearly an hour to deliberate before awarding first place to Peggy. Kimberly, a stunner who parlayed her willowy blonde looks into doing Washington state college sports reports for ESPN, never got over it.

"Hey, Silver, I hear you've been calling around Mt. Vernon asking to talk to people. And you don't call me?"

"You're one of my bridesmaids, Kimberly. Why would I torture myself calling you when I'll be seeing you in New York soon enough?"

"Ah, honey, you know I give you a hard time only because I love you."

"What's with calling me 'Silver?' Won't you ever stop grousing that the judges robbed you at States?"

"I *was* robbed. And I want you to give me the gold medal. I'll give you the silver medal I've been holding for you."

"I'm renting a fur coat for you for the wedding, that should appease you, right?"

"Nothing short of justice will appease me. I want my gold medal."

"You work for ESPN; you should be able to get someone to make you a replica of the gold medal. You can attach it to a pacifier and wear it around your neck."

"Haha, now that's an idea. Maybe I'll wear the silver medal around my neck at your wedding to showcase the injustice."

"Big hug, sweetheart. Kidding aside, I'm looking forward to seeing you at the wedding."

"You'll recognize me. I'll be wearing your silver medal."

"Actually, I do have an idea about that. We'll talk soon. Adios!"

Closing day on their condo finally arrived after Peggy and Michael put the deal back on schedule. While they waited for three o'clock — the time of the bank appointment — to arrive, they sat at the kitchen table in her condo drinking tea and talking about progress with the Anniversary Box search.

"From all that we've learned so far, Michael, what do you believe is the secret to make love last a lifetime?"

"I'll go with the answer George Harrison gives in 'What is Life?'"

"Maybe I should just go to Craig's List and search for a groom under 'Wise Ass.'"

"I'm not kidding. George's song makes it clear to me that without you, my life would be a wasteland."

"You say you love me, but what would make you love me for a lifetime? And be serious."

"I would love you forever if I knew you always had my back."

"Now, we're getting somewhere. Tell me more."

"You know what I'm talking about."

"I want to hear it from you. What do you mean 'have your back'?"

"Knowing that you would risk losing something of great value, for me."

"Explain."

"That you would give up something of great importance to you, and that you'd do it for me if I had a need."

"Keep going."

"I'm an accountant, man. I'm not a talker."

"You are now, keep going."

"In high school, a teacher told the class a story about a man who fell into a deep hole and was stuck. He couldn't get out. An acquaintance walked by, saw the man struggling, and told him to hang on. 'I'll call someone to help you,' he said. Then a while later, a parishioner from the man's church walked by and said, 'Oh, my, you are in a tough way. I will pray for you.' A while later, a true friend walked by and jumped into the hole. 'Wait,' the man said. 'Why did you do that, now we're both in a hole!' And the true friend said, 'Yes, but I've been in a hole like this before, and I know the way out.'"

She looked at him, seeing him in a new light. One she really liked.

"I've never told that to anyone before. But that's what I mean by 'have my back.' I don't always know what motivates me. But I do know what scares me — and that is the thought of ever losing you."

"I love how you always continue to surprise me on the upside, Michael."

He looked at her, seeing her on a deeper level as well.

"I'll always have your back," she said.

"That's how we bring this courtship home, isn't it?"

She put her hand on top of his, when suddenly his phone pinged, indicating a message had just come in. A moment later, he popped out of his chair and let out a "Wooohoooo!" that shook the rafters, and Peggy sat up startled.

"Look at this," he said, and he leaned over to show her his phone. "I just got an email from Phil Mickelson's agent inviting me to play a practice round of golf in Florida with Phil at some point."

"Wow!" she said. "That's so cool!"

"Must have been the fire chief who came through for me. I've been bustin' my butt on that account. Can you believe this? I'm so stoked, bay-beeeee!"

She gave him a congratulatory hug when her phone rang. It was another one of her mom's friends calling. Her name was Sue, the owner of the town's art-supplies store. Sue said she had heard through the grapevine that Peggy was looking for "Joanie stories."

"Your mom had a famous expression, 'We may never pass this way again,'" Sue said. She asked if she was calling at a good time, as it was obvious from her tone that she could hear Michael carrying on in the background with a continuous stream of "Woooohooos."

"I have a little boy who just had Christmas come early," Peggy said, "but I have time. Go ahead and talk, I'll step into a soundproof booth."

Sue told how Peggy's mom and dad embraced the idea of creating experiences that could be savored as memories.

"They would take off on the spur of the moment to the San Juan Islands. 'Ferry days,' they called their drop-everything-and-go trips. If the day was bright and blue, they'd cancel their appointments and hop in the car. They'd drive to the ferry to spend the day riding it from Anacortes to Friday Harbor — and back — just to stand on the top deck and watch the glassy water slide by, the clouds roll past, and the seagulls circle overhead. They loved to do things together that could make memories."

Peggy finished up her call with Sue and prepared to leave for the bank with Michael, who finally came down from his orbit. But first, she asked him to help her roll up the rug in her living room. It was an eight by six, handmade Tibetan rug designed by her mom's artist friend, Dale Gottlieb, a famous designer. It had reds and yellows in a splash like a sunset and an inscription at the top in Dale's script that read, "My heart sings." Her mom had loved the rug, and it was one of the few items Peggy had kept before selling her parents' house.

"What's the story with the rug?" Michael asked, as he watched her take up a corner.

"I know we're not moving into our new place until after the wedding, but once we do the closing, I want to bring the rug to the condo to see how it will look in the living room," she said, and he nodded, signaling that her reasoning made sense.

It was late afternoon by the time they completed the paperwork at the bank, and he carried one end of the rug in the front door of their new condo as she walked through the door holding the other end.

"Rug looks great," Michael said as they spread it out on the polished oak floor, and it gave a bright flash of color to the barren room to match the sunset through the window.

"I loved Sue's story today," Peggy said, as she stepped closer to Michael and let one of her thighs touch his.

"I liked the message, too — that we may never pass this way again. But I suspect we'll be in this living room a lot," he said, not getting her drift, but not disliking that she was sidling up to him.

"We'll never pass this way again," she whispered in his ear, as she undid his tie.

"What are you trying to tell me?"

"We'll be in this living room again. But we'll never be in the living room for the first time again."

Now he understood where she was going, and he used his finger to trace a line along her cheek. "You suggesting something?"

"I'm suggesting we communicate with each other non-verbally what a great memory this could be," she said, as her hands slid down a little lower.

"Guess I can see now why you wanted to bring the rug."

"I'm talking to you, Mr. Crazytown," she said, whispering.

That's the last thing she said verbally before they dropped to their knees, lay on the "My heart sings" rug, wrapped arms and legs around each other, and communicated their excitement at being in their new home for the first time.

Chapter Eight

"**H**igh touch, high talk."

It was a topic raised by another one of her mom's friends, Diane, a hair stylist.

"'You can't have sex every night, but it's not a bad goal,' your mom used to say," said Diane. "I've tried that with my Freddie. Smokes his brains out now that he can get marijuana at the corner store. But my promptings have had a positive impact on his inertia, somewhat."

Diane added an important coda to the thesis. "But your mom believed that husband and wife should strive to engage in conversation with equal passion, and conversation should be heart to heart.

No empty words to fill time and space. I've had a harder time with my Freddie on that one."

Another friend, Carolyn, remembered another entry in the Anniversary Box: "No passive aggression allowed."

"Not a strong suit with your mom, but she did try to temper herself."

"Tell me," Peggy said, as she caught up to Carolyn for a Zoom session. The expansive green fields of Skagit County farmland filled the background out the window as Carolyn spoke from her farmhouse. Carolyn was a berry canner, and one of her mom's marathon training partners.

"Your mom and dad were very different. Declan could take the knocks, while Joanie bruised easily. Sometimes, we wouldn't know for a week or two that we had hurt her feelings. If one of us said something she perceived as hurtful, she'd remain silent. Then a week or two later, she'd hit us with a broadside. 'Where did that come from?' I'd say. 'Two weeks ago you said such and such,' she'd say."

"Got an example?"

"One time, a group of us went out for a six-mile run. Chrissy, one of the girls, said something about art in school being a waste. Chrissy's very right-wing and thinks schools should focus only on the subjects that can be measured in economic terms. Taxpayer funds should go to measurable endeavors, that kind of attitude.

"Two weeks later, we were at a beverage store on the trail after finishing our run, and your mom asked if anyone wanted a drink. We all said yes, and she went into the store, but when she came out, she had a bottle of Gatorade for everyone except Chrissy.

"'What am I, chopped liver?' Chrissy said, and your mom said, 'You dissed art.'

"Joan was very sensitive. But she understood that about herself and she did work to tone it down. Sometimes, though, the devil on her left shoulder won out over the angel on her right shoulder. Chrissy paid the price in that example, but it would happen to your dad, too. We'd be out for dinner at a restaurant, me, my Dan, Joanie, and your dad. Suddenly, pow! She'd hit your dad with a zinger out of the blue. He was well-conditioned, though, and he'd take it in stride. 'What did I do now, two weeks ago?' he'd say with a smile. Joan and Declan would laugh it off, and she'd offer to pay for their next Coors-beer-and-pizza session. It was amazing how they rolled with the punches. I never saw them use a harsh word with each other, not in the top-of-the-lungs way my Dan and I could go at it."

Amy, her mom's acupuncturist, told how her mom's sensitivity gave her an ability to see things others could not see.

"Once we were in the car on the way to Seattle. There was a new hand-painted fabric store your mom wanted me to see," said Amy. "I was driving, and your mom said, 'Watch out for that asshole in the blue Volvo. He changes lanes without signaling.' I asked her how she knew that. 'I saw him in Marysville do it three times,' she said, and I said, 'But that was forty miles ago. How can you remember a car from forty miles back?' Sure enough though, a minute later, the blue Volvo nearly brushed up against another car at seventy miles an hour, and thank God I listened to your mom and had backed off tailing the guy. Otherwise, we would have had a major wreck on I-5. Your mom had special insight, for sure, and I remember your dad would often say, 'Some people talk to tell, but when Joanie talks, I listen to learn.'"

On a sales trip to Atlanta the next week, Peggy finished up a meeting early and booked a flight to Ft. Lauderdale before returning home to New York.

She wanted to see her dad's cousin, Father Pat. He served as Chaplin to the Broward County School Board based in Ft. Lauderdale and he was very close to the family. He was scheduled to marry her and Michael, and Peggy wanted to talk to him in person to gain his wise counsel as a surrogate for her dad. When she called from Atlanta, he invited her to meet him at his office in Ft. Lauderdale as soon as she got to town.

"Declan saved the schools a ton of money. He had an ability to spot a problem and sum it up in twenty-five words or less," Father Pat said.

Her dad had created his own educational consulting firm after serving in various senior administrative roles at colleges during his younger years. After gaining experience, he combined that with a *Chronicle of Higher Education* front-page feature on his organizing ability and started his own consulting business.

"He came to Florida often for his work. I'm grateful he was able to see so much of you," Peggy said. "He always told me how happy that made him."

"Declan had a special talent, with one small quirk. He had a tendency to call a horse's ass a horse's ass."

"I think I got that gene."

Father Pat laughed. "He got the important stuff right, though. He stepped up when your mom got sick."

"He did double duty during those four years, not only taking care of my mom, but keeping his business going."

"One time, we were in the middle of a complicated project. The Board had to reorder administrative functions between our junior high schools and high schools, and they needed your dad for a meeting. He caught a red-eye from Seattle to do a presentation, then caught the next red-eye home to take your mom to chemo."

Peggy had been in school in California during much of her mom's illness, but she remembered clearly the strain it had put on her dad.

"I'm sure stress played a role in his health," Father Pat said, referring to her dad's stroke. "I'd ask him about it, how things must get hard at times, and he'd say, 'Joanie never complains.' They had a special bond. I'm sure you're as curious as I am about how they were able to stay so strong as a couple."

"I am, that's why I'm here. I recently learned that my parents had an Anniversary Box. Each year, they would write a message to affirm their bond."

"I know."

"You do?"

"Your dad talked about the Anniversary Box. He got very excited as each anniversary approached, to see what new thing they could come up with."

"Do you recall any stories?"

"'Adversity is a teacher — listen to the teacher.' I remember that one," Father Pat said, and he sat back in his chair and smiled. "Your dad was very eloquent on the topic. He said the struggle he and your mom had early in their relationship made them stronger. I asked him if I could borrow that theme for my sermon on Sunday."

"That's why I want to find the Anniversary Box.

I'll be getting married to Michael soon, as you know, and I want to know how to keep love alive."

"Your dad told me he and your mom were working on an entry for their twenty-fifth. Sadly, she died shortly before that milestone anniversary."

"Yes, three weeks before."

"Your dad was excited because it was their twenty-fifth, and he wanted to write something special with your mom to crystallize everything about their life together, the secret, as you call it. He said he wanted to capture the essence of how they were able to bridge the divide of separateness."

"The divide of separateness?"

"He was consumed with the concept. He believed that separateness was a temporal manifestation, as he put it, and he believed he and Joanie had bridged that divide. Later at your mom's memorial service, he told me he had finished his story."

"Really? He wrote something to my mom after she passed away?"

"It's not just the twenty-four messages in that box, Peggy. I'm thinking if you find the box, you may find a story for their twenty-fifth anniversary that pulls it all together. I suspect everything you've been looking for in terms of understanding how two people can create an unbreakable bond is in that final letter."

She thanked Father Pat and checked her watch to make sure she had time to get to the airport to catch her flight to New York. She wanted to get home so she could be on time for work the next day and keep Hal happy.

Father Pat hugged her as she got up to leave. "I hope you find the box, Peggy. It would be your dad and mom's gift to you."

In the Uber on the way to the airport, she got a message from Doug Phillips, the pharma lobbyist, and she returned his call.

"Sorry, but I don't have good news," he said. "I've been shot down trying to find the right guy to talk to about getting your dad on the philanthropic program. I'm sorry I couldn't help. I'll keep trying, but I did want to keep you posted that I haven't had any luck, so far."

She thanked him for his effort, only to have his downer news compounded when she got to the airport and learned that her flight had been canceled. She hurried to the Customer Service desk to rebook, but as she waited in line, a text came in. It was from Hal.

"Nobody told you to go to Florida. Don't bother coming in tomorrow."

She called Michael.

"I have bad news, too," he said. "We just lost the San Francisco account, and I've been laid off."

She was silent.

"Honey, you still there?"

"Yes," she said as she pondered the new lesson she had just learned from Father Pat:

Adversity is a teacher — listen to the teacher.

Chapter Nine

She called Hal the next morning, but he refused to take her call. She kept calling until she finally got through to him at about noon.

"What do you mean, you're firing me?"

As she listened to his one-way opus on how she had "transgressed" going to Florida without his permission, images of financial ruin ran through her head, mixed with strategies to fend it off, including doing an inventory of friends who might be able to help her find a new job — fast.

The mail that had accumulated while she had been away sat on the kitchen counter. As Hal barked on and on, she sorted through the mail to distract herself.

With one hand, she held the phone away from her ear, with the other, she leafed through envelopes. As Hal listed all the ways she was "unprofessional," she spied a bill from a storage company in Mt. Vernon, Washington, with the subject on the envelope, "Art Room Valuables."

Art Room Valuables?

"This is the last straw," Hal said, his tone marked by its rankling insincerity. "As much as I'd like to help you, there is nothing I can do to salvage this situation."

"Your loss," she said, and she punched the red dot on her phone to end the call. Then she opened the storage company letter.

The message was direct: "You have not paid your balance; therefore we have no option but to clear out the contents of your unit." She read a bit further, "Action to dispose of your items will happen three days from the date of this letter."

It had taken three days for the letter to reach her, which meant clearing out the unit was set to happen that day, or possibly had happened already.

She called Michael and read the letter to him.

"Who is it addressed to?" he said.

She looked more closely. "My dad," she said. "That makes sense since all his mail gets forwarded to me. But I don't know anything about a storage unit."

"It's noon here, 9:00 a.m. their time. Call the number on the letter and ask what's up."

She got a person on the first ring, a young lady by the sound of the voice. "Cascade Heated Storage."

"I just received a letter saying my storage unit is in default."

"Customer number, please," said the young lady, who directed Peggy to a number in the top right corner of the letter.

Peggy gave the number, and after a pause that included the sound of computer keys being punched, the young lady said, "Declan Moore?"

"That's right," Peggy said. "Can you tell me the situation?"

The young lady read the note posted in the computer: "The unit owner opened an account three years ago for our smallest unit, three by six. Unit owner titled it 'Art Room Valuables' and paid for a full year at the time of opening. But the system did not pick up on the renewal at the end of that first year, and bookkeeping failed to bill Declan Moore. Now the account is seriously delinquent.

"The unit is scheduled to be cleaned out today," said the young lady. "The crew is on its way now."

"What do I owe you to keep it open?"

Again, the sound of computer keys being punched. "$1,278."

Peggy took a credit card from her wallet and paid the fee, which put her at the upper limit of available credit on that card, but it solved the issue.

Peggy called Michael and told him. "I'm going to fly out to Washington today to check on my dad's storage unit. He called the account Art Room Valuables."

"You're going today?"

"My Aunt Eileen told me my mom kept the Anniversary Box in her art room. The box may be in that unit, Michael. I don't have a job, so I'm going."

"I'll go with you. I don't have a job either."

"You'd do that for me?"

"Not me. We," he said, and she smiled, reaffirmed in the wisdom of her choice to love him.

A man in overalls walked Peggy and Michael to the third floor of the storage building where the unit was located. As he fidgeted with the lock on the unit door to break it, she tried to anticipate what might await them inside.

And hoped!

The man in overalls opened the door, and she and Michael took out knives to open the dozen or so boxes. Mostly, they found art books, sketch pads, and press clippings highlighting her mom's gallery showings, as well as financial records, including tax returns and receipts for her mom's business.

But no Anniversary Box.

"You need me to stay?" said the man in overalls.

"We're looking for something specific," Peggy said. "We don't see it yet, but we're going to keep looking."

"Suit yourself. That'll be $22.15, with tax, when you're ready to have me put a new lock back on this baby."

An hour later, after scouring the unit fully, they sat on a bench in the storage unit courtyard and didn't speak for a long time.

"I was so hoping," she said.

Michael mentioned they might want to visit the moving company in town that had shipped her parents' things east. He suggested the mover could give them a price for moving the files from the storage unit to New York rather than sustain an ongoing monthly charge.

Ah, ever the accountant! She agreed that was a good idea.

"Plus we can ask Pete—the moving company owner's name is Pete—if he might still be holding items from the shipment that got sent east."

"A long shot," Michael said, "but worth a try."

Pete gave Peggy a big hug when she stepped into the moving company office. He and her dad had been members of the same running group in Mt. Vernon.

She got right to the point. "Pete, since you moved my folks' stuff east, I learned they had a thing called an Anniversary Box." She took out her phone and showed him the photo she'd taken of her Aunt Eileen's painting of the box.

"Looks lovely," Pete said.

"We're hoping there are items from their house that, by some miracle, got left behind and possibly the Anniversary Box might still be here."

He took them to a back area of the warehouse.

"This is the cubicle where we stored your mom and

dad's stuff before shipping things out. As you can see, it's clean as a whistle." She was sure the look on Michael's face mirrored her own. Crestfallen. "Sorry to disappoint, but hey, there's always a possibility that someone might have seen something. I'd be happy to ask around."

That night she took Michael to LaFiamma, the pizza place in Bellingham, the next town over, which she had frequented as a ritual on so many Friday nights with her parents while growing up.

Tad, the owner, seated them at her parents' favorite table by the window.

"You're very quiet," Michael said.

"I'm thinking back to all the memories at this table."

"Are you disappointed that we came all the way to Washington only to come up empty on the Anniversary Box?"

"You're sitting in my mom's seat, Michael. One Friday night, I was very sad. I had lost a close race that afternoon, and I fought hard not to show it. But my mom could see it in my face, and she asked me if I was upset about the race. I told her it didn't bother me. She took my hand and looked into my eyes. 'The you sitting in front of me is okay,' she said. 'That you will do just fine in life. But the you that is inside you, the one only you can see, has greatness inside her, if you choose to tap it.'"

"What did she mean by that?"

"It's natural to cover up hurt, she said, to put a shield over pain. But it takes courage to let people see us when we are hurting. 'The you inside you, the one nobody can see, has a great capacity to feel,' she said. 'If you accept the risk of that and let others see you for who you are, that will unlock the secret. If you feel what you feel, and you're not afraid to show your heart to the world, you will live a rich and full life.'"

"I wish I'd had a mom like that sitting across from me when I was growing up."

"Coming all this way for nothing and coming up empty on the Anniversary Box, yes, it hurts like hell."

Tad brought their pizza, but before he took a bite, Michael said, "That's why I love you."

"Why?"

"Because you let me see your heart."

The next morning, after taking a group of her mom's friends to breakfast to thank them for helping track down stories, she and Michael were driving back to the airport hotel to pack up before flying home when she got a call from Pete.

"Got good news and bad news," he said. "Good news is one of the line guys who helped load items from your parents' house says he remembers seeing the Anniversary Box."

"Bad news?"

"Bad news is he says he threw it out."

They rushed over as quickly as they could to meet with Pete and the college kid who worked for the moving company and recalled the box. The kid had long hair and big muscles under a tight Led Zeppelin T-shirt.

"I remember the box," he said.

"This one?" she said, and she showed him the photo on her phone.

"Yup, that's it. Before putting a rug and some cartons and things on the truck to bring over here and prepare them for shipping out, we made a dump run."

"You made a dump run that day?"

"Yeah, there were garbage bags and cracked plates and stuff in the kitchen, but also trash in the art room. One of the homeowners musta been an artist because there was a room with dried out paints and busted canvases and other trash. We loaded up the trash for a dump run. I remember thinking it was odd that a

fancy wooden box would be in the trash, but it was —
and so out it went with the other rubbish."

Again, she showed him the photo. "You're sure it
was *this* wooden box?"

"I'm, like, 99.9% sure."

Michael glanced at Peggy. *Not good,* both of their
expressions said.

The college kid said he was sorry if he did anything
wrong, but they told him not to worry.

Peggy gave him a twenty dollar bill, and he shook
her hand.

Pete waited until the kid was gone, then said to
Peggy, "He's a good kid, but he's a kid. Mostly has
girls on his mind and the spread on the Seahawks/
Dallas game. So, don't give up hope. He could be
wrong."

She looked at the floor and shook her head.

Adversity is a teacher! But, man, doesn't the teacher
ever take a holiday?

The next morning after returning from Washington,

she got in the car and drove to Norwalk to see her dad, where the home's administrator ran up to her with "exciting news."

"We got a letter this morning from one of the pharma companies that offers drugs for the 'locked-in' trials, and your dad has been accepted."

The administrator could hardly speak, she was so excited, as she showed Peggy the letter, which said: "We're pleased to announce that Declan Moore has been accepted into our philanthropic program to receive a trial drug for one year. The $10,000 monthly fee will be waived during this period."

Peggy and the woman hugged, turning a circle or two. "They will start him on a protocol next month. Isn't that exciting? We don't know if he feels anguish at being in this state, but now we can have certainty we're providing him with the best of care," the administrator said.

"Yes. But how did this happen? Who made it happen?"

"We don't know. The letter just came in the mail."

It was a gorgeous blue-sky day, and the nurses dressed her dad in a red sweater to celebrate the red-letter day. They seated him in a wheelchair with a plaid blanket on his lap so she could wheel him around the grounds to take advantage of the wonderful weather.

She stopped by a stone wall with a pond beyond. She sat on the wall as she faced him and told him the good news about the trial drug that would start soon, and she peered into his eyes. "Isn't that so exciting? If the drug works, we will know for sure that we're doing everything we can for you. Oh, that will be such a relief!"

Her dad continued to stare at her vaguely, and she took his hand.

"Dad, I've been talking to your friends to learn about your Anniversary Box. I have learned so many wonderful stories about you and Mom. I came here today because I want you to know you and Mom are still well-loved in Washington."

His blue eyes were wide open. She smiled at him, hoping he could see her on some level.

"I learned about 'Not me. We.' I learned how you and Mom sought out experiences so you could share them as memories. Most of all, the message I love best, because it's one I knew from my own experience with you is, 'Coors beer and pizza.' That's my favorite, since I got to share so many trips to pizza places with you both. I learned to value conversation, a habit I have absorbed into my being on a cellular level, thanks to you.

"But most of all, what I learned talking to your friends is how you taught others by your strong example. People watched you, Dad. They saw the respect you showed Mom, and they integrated that into their own lives. That's a powerful legacy."

The wind stirred, and she rearranged the blanket on his lap.

"What I wanted to learn most on my journey was how two people keep love alive. How does a couple make their love last a lifetime?"

She paused as she brushed back a shock of hair from his forehead.

"Respect is part of it. But so is playfulness. I love the PayDay story."

She paused to see if his eyes remained focused over her shoulder. They did, yet she continued.

"Mom was in bed full-time by that point. One night out of the blue, she asked you to buy her a PayDay candy bar. Her dad, who died when she was in college, used to buy her PayDay candy bars when she was a little girl for their walks around Castle Island. You understood how important that memory was to her, so you drove around town until you found a Rite Aid that had candy. They had one bag of miniature PayDays left. Mom took a bite out of the tiny bar and left the rest on her nightstand, but you were happy because you had made her happy. You went into the kitchen and you opened a PayDay for yourself. They were small, so you had another. Then another.

Suddenly, Mom called out from the bedroom, 'Stop eating my PayDays!' With candy in your mouth, you said, 'I'm not eating your PayDays,' and you crossed your fingers like a six-year-old hoping to negate the lie. 'Yes, you are!' she called out again, and you said, 'How would you know? You're in the other room.' And she said, 'Because I can hear you opening the wrappers!' Oh, she could be a tough cookie, as we know, but you guys clicked. That's why I'm telling you all this, Dad. That's a gift I received. By learning more about you and Mom, I've learned more about myself."

She moved closer, leaning in from the cobblestone wall, and she looked into his eyes.

"I love Michael, and I want to be fully connected to him. That's why I set out to look for the Anniversary Box. I'm so sorry the box is lost and I will never see the stories. I will never see the handwritten notes you and Mom wrote to each other to affirm your love and take steps each year to strengthen your bond. But just knowing the stories existed has given me hope that I can achieve the same level of connection with Michael that you did with Mom. I never told you this enough, Dad, but I'm proud to be your daughter."

A long moment passed, and she saw something, or thought she did, below his right eye.

Could it be? Could it be real?

A tear?

She touched his face, and his skin was moist below his right eye as she traced the winding path of a single tear down his cheek.

"You heard me, Dad! All this time, you've been hearing me! Oh, my God!"

She leaned across his chair to hug him. She wanted to hold on and never let go.

Chapter Ten

She told Michael about her dad's tear, and he was ecstatic for her. She told him about the good news from the pharma company, getting accepted by their philanthropic program, but for some reason, though he was clearly excited, he did not look surprised.

"That's $10,000 savings a month, Michael. You're an accountant. A hundred and twenty grand a year."

"I think it's fabulous. I'm sure it's a result of the many thousands of letters you wrote. You're incredible how you never give up."

"It's the impossible dream come true."

"Yes, it is, and I have good news, too."

He shared his news that a major accounting firm had called him, eager to hire him, and it looked like he might have a job by the end of the week.

She told him about three friends who had leads on jobs for her. They shared a high-five as they climbed into the car to head out to complete some of the tasks on their wedding checklist, confident now that they could go ahead with the wedding and not have to worry so much about money.

"I'm happy I did not call the people on the wedding invitation list during my P.O.P.," she said as they drove to the fur-coat rental place to attend to the first task on the check list.

"P.O.P.?"

"My Pissed-off Phase."

"Oh, yeah, I remember that."

"Now we don't have to call everybody back to tell them the wedding is on again, because to them, it was never off."

"A bit of twisted logic, but yes," he said, as he

pulled into the parking lot at the rental shop. "Did you call ahead to order the coats?"

"I did. They're holding three coats for the girls, plus one for me. Three of the bridesmaids already have their own coats to wear."

They stood at the counter, and the saleslady brought out four fur coats and hung them on a hook so they could inspect them.

Peggy went to pay to reserve them for pick-up the day before the wedding, but Michael said, "No, let me do this."

"Really?"

"Give each other gifts," he said. "There's something to this Anniversary Box thing."

As they pulled out of the parking lot to head to their next chore on the list, Peggy's cell phone rang. She reached for her pocketbook on the floor on the passenger side to answer it.

Listening for a moment, she suddenly exclaimed, "Oh, no! My God, no!"

Instinctively, Michael pulled the car to the side of the road and shifted into park. "What is it?"

"My dad," she said. "He's just had another stroke."

Peggy put the phone on speaker as the nurse told her it was serious. "Doctors are here already. You should hurry."

Michael spun the car around and headed for the parkway that would take them to the Throggs Neck Bridge and the Bronx. They sped through the Bronx toward the Connecticut Turnpike heading to Norwalk, but as soon as they got to Mamaroneck, fourteen miles away still, traffic slowed to a crawl, then stopped entirely. She checked her cellphone to see if she could learn anything.

"Oh, Christ! A tractor trailer jackknifed at the New York/Connecticut line. We're going to be here for hours!"

Michael got off the highway at Rye, and they pulled into the parking lot at the MTA train station. They waited on the platform for twelve minutes for a train heading north, an eternity, and then the first one to arrive was a local, so it made every stop.

When they finally got to Norwalk, they called an Uber that took them to the nursing home. It dropped them off at the front door, but as she raced for the door, a nurse stepped out and put up her hands in a gesture to stop.

"You dad's on his way to the hospital. The ambulance just left."

The nursing home administrator appeared and held up her car keys.

"Come with me, I'll give you a ride."

At the Emergency Room front desk they learned that her dad was already in surgery. They took seats in the waiting room until a doctor appeared, three hours later, and announced that her dad was out of surgery.

"He's in intensive care. If you follow me, you can see him through the window."

She stood in the hallway, fingertips of both hands

pressed to the glass. She stared at her dad as he lay very still with IVs in his arms on both sides of the bed.

Michael stepped up behind her and held her close.

Back home, she sat in a chair by her bed and stared at the wall. It went like that for a day, then two, then three. Each afternoon, she'd take a trip up to the hospital to sit in the lobby with Michael. She wanted to be close to her dad, even though she couldn't see him except through the intensive care window. Every few hours, the doctors would come out to the lobby to offer the same report.

"It's still too early to tell."

In the evening at home, she'd open new cards that had come in the mail that day, cards wishing her and Michael good cheer on their wedding. The wedding was still a bit more than two weeks off, but all she could do was stare at the cards and feel numb.

"Maybe we should postpone the wedding," Michael said.

"I don't know what to do," she said. "I don't know what to do."

On the fourth day, she received a text from the administrator at her dad's nursing home.

"Call me," the note said.

When Peggy called, she learned that a nurse who had worked on her dad's team had been on vacation the day of her dad's stroke. The nurse had just returned to work and had something important to report.

"I was so sorry to hear about your dad," the nurse said, when she got on the phone. "We're all praying for him."

"Thank you," Peggy said.

"I'm the one who gave you the blanket to put on your dad's lap the day you came to visit last week. You took him for a walk in his wheelchair, and I wanted him to be warm."

"Yes, I remember. Thank you."

"Your dad seemed very agitated after you left. I put him back in bed, but it was like he was trying to tell me something."

"How do you mean?"

"It was strange, because generally he is so mild. But he was agitated that evening. I pointed to the books on the shelf by his bed, thinking maybe he wanted me to read to him. But no, that didn't do any good. He remained agitated until I touched that Scrabble game you brought for him on one of your trips."

"And?"

"I opened the box and took out all the little wooden letters and spread them out across his lap. That calmed him down. He had a hard time moving his hands, as you know, and he struggled with that as he pointed to the letters. After half an hour, he had singled out four letters."

"Really? Which ones?"

"T, S, U and C."

Peggy remained silent, waiting for the nurse to talk. "I went on vacation the next day, but I kept the letters, thinking I could give them to you the next time I saw you. But now that your dad is back in the hospital, I thought I should call you. Would you like to come up and get the letters?"

"Yes, absolutely. We'll be up right away," Peggy said.

"I kept them in a napkin for you. I don't know what they mean, but I think your dad wanted you to have these letters."

Peggy and Michael drove up to get the letters, and when they returned to her apartment around dinner time, they spread them out on her kitchen table: T, S, U and C.

"What do you make of these?" Michael asked, as she prepared dinner and he scrambled the letters trying to form different words.

They sat at the table for many hours after finishing their meal, not talking — just thinking — playing with different permutations.

Peggy arranged the letters so they spelled SUTC and said, "Maybe we're missing some letters. Maybe we're missing a vowel or two."

She went to her Scrabble game on a shelf in the living room and returned with a set of vowels. She added an A and an E then an I. She used the I to form "SUITC." Again they stared at the letters, until Peggy suddenly sat up straight and shouted, "Holy shit!"

"What?"

"Suitcase!"

"What suitcase?"

"Come with me," she said. She ran for the stairs and raced into the attic with Michael hot on her heels.

Up in the attic, she moved boxes until she got to the suitcase, the one her dad had packed for her mom for the last trip to Seattle they never took. She tried to open the suitcase, but it was locked. She went to her mom's box marked "Save — Special Photos" and sorted through the pictures till she found the anthology she'd given them that included "The Gift of the Magi." She opened the book to the back cover to get the key taped inside the back flap.

She took the key and tried it on the suitcase.

Presto! It opened the lock.

Carefully, she sorted through her mom's clothes packed neatly in plastic bags to keep them fresh — her mom's patented approach — sorting through slacks, blouses, and a nightgown — until she came to a bulky item. Wrapped in a fine felt cloth was a polished wooden box with a rose on the front — the Anniversary Box.

She opened it as Michael moved in close, and they sorted through the cards with numbers on them:

1) Build on what we've built.

2) It takes two to make "one" work.

3) Not me, we!

4) Love means saying you're sorry.

5) When you win, I win.

The whole assortment of twenty-four messages her parents had written to each other were there.

"Makes perfect sense that the box would be in the suitcase, since they had planned to work on their twenty-fifth anniversary message when they got to the Seattle hotel," she said.

She and Michael continued to read through the entries, then as she came to an envelope marked "Number 25," she paused. Slowly, she opened the envelope to remove the letter inside.

It was the letter her dad had written to her mom on what would have been their twenty-fifth anniversary. He had titled it, "The Gift of the Magi Principle."

She started to read it, and Michael took her hand.

But as she read further, she started to cry, first softly, then inconsolably, and Michael reached his arm around her shoulders to pull her tight.

"I've got to see him," she said.

"It's so late."

"I've got to see him now."

It was near midnight as they drove to the hospital. On the way up they connected on the phone with a doctor on the night shift who said he'd meet them in the lobby.

He was a new doctor, someone she hadn't met before. He had rich brown eyes, and she saw a light in his eyes as a smile crossed his lips.

"I wanted to meet you at the door," he said. "I have good news."

She leaned forward, her eyes wide.

"Your dad is responding."

"Tell me."

The doctor took both her hands in his. "He's awake. He's stable."

"I need to see him."

The doctor led Peggy and Michael down a long corridor to an elevator bank, where a thought occurred to her: *give to get*.

That was an expression her dad would often say when she was a young girl. He never pushed the point, he simply lived by it, the idea that if we give in life, when we need it, life will pay us back. The divine will recognize us for all that we have "given," and when we need it most, we will "get."

"I understand you have a pharma company that has offered to provide your dad with a drug for a trial," the doctor said, as they waited for the elevator doors to open.

"Yes, the protocol is set to start next month."

"I think you will be happy."

"Tell me."

"I think your dad will be able to do that trial."

They stepped into the elevator, and she reached into her purse for her dad's letter, "Number 25."

All was empty and quiet on the corridor as the doctor led them to a room at the far end of the hall. As she turned the corner and entered the room, she saw her dad lying in bed with his eyes open.

She stepped to the foot of the bed so she could look at him straight on.

His eyes didn't move, they remained focused in space, as she held up the envelope, "Number 25," and she set the four wooden letters from the Scrabble game — T, S, U, C — on the bed. She smiled as she put the letter, "The Gift of the Magi Principle," and herself into his line of sight.

"This is beautiful, what you wrote about Mom."

He continued to look at her, and she knew he could see her.

Chapter Eleven

Two weeks later, the night before the wedding, the wedding party gathered at Prost, a tavern on Franklin Avenue. They told Michael and Peggy stories, roasting entwined with toasting and laughter, and they saluted members of the party who had come a long distance to be there. The top award went to bridesmaid Kimberly, who flew in from Washington state, but several of Michael's friends wanted credit for coming in on the train from Brooklyn.

Michael's best man, Charlie, claimed he should get credit for traveling in from New Jersey. "I needed to bring my passport," he said, and the group shared fist bumps.

The talk turned to golf, Michael's favorite sport, and someone made the point that Garden City was near Bethpage, where the U.S. Open was set to be played the next year. One of the groomsmen asked Michael if he regretted giving up his chance to play a round of golf with Phil Mickelson.

"You had an invitation to play with Phil Mickelson?" said two guys in unison.

Peggy chipped in. "Not 'had.' He *has* an invitation to play a practice round with Phil Mickelson in Florida next month."

"No, you're wrong, Peggy," said Charlie. "He traded his invitation."

"Traded?"

"Yeah, he gave it to some guy at a pharma company who could pitch his philanthropic colleagues to approve free use of a drug for a trial."

Peggy took Michael by the arm and pulled him to the side. "That was you? You did that?"

"It was nothing, really. The invitation to play with

Mickelson came out of nowhere anyway."

"You did that for my dad, Michael. You did that for me."

"The invitation came out of the blue, sweetie. Most likely from the fire chief. If it came once, it'll come again. As Tug McGraw said about the '73 Mets, 'You gotta believe.'"

Kimberly joined the group, carrying margaritas in both hands and wearing a gold medal on a ribbon around her neck.

"Hey, what do we have here?" said Charlie, "The gold-medal winner in the Margarita 10K, the two-fisted division?"

"I thought you were the silver-medal winner in high school?" Michael said, adopting a frown.

"I'm the gold-medal winner. Ask Peggy," Kimberly said, puffing up her chest so the gold medal could show prominently. "I promised her I'd wear my medal at her wedding."

"What do you mean 'my' medal. Peggy has the

gold medal."

"She did," said another of the bridesmaids who relieved Kimberly of one of her margaritas. "Peggy traded the gold."

"What do you mean 'traded'?" Michael asked.

The bridesmaid raised her margarita to salute Peggy and Kimberly. "Peggy gave Kimberly the gold medal, and Kimberly put the arm on a guy in her office at ESPN to get Peggy a golf invitation."

The wheels turned inside Michael's brain, as he processed the data, until the tally was made and the score flashed across his face like big numbers on a leader board. This time, he took Peggy by the arm and pulled her aside.

They stared at each other a long moment, as Kimberly stepped between them to give Peggy a smooch on the cheek before scooting away. "Told you I'd tease you."

Peggy and Michael continued to stare at each other, then he edged her toward a section of the bar where it was quieter and he looked deep into her eyes. Each of their smiles started small around the corners of their lips, then expanded full across their faces.

"You did that for me with Mickelson?"

Peggy shrugged. "I heard you like golf."

"Will you marry me?"

"Will canoodling be involved?"

"I hope so."

"What would the bike people say?"

"Tell them, 'I do.'"

"Now you've got my attention."

Guests streamed into St Joseph's Church for the wedding the next day on a crystal blue afternoon. Men wore suits, and women fanned out in colorful dresses like the view through a kaleidoscope.

Peggy looked gorgeous in her mom's wedding veil, which descended gracefully across the shoulders of her gown. Her bridesmaids gathered around her for an impromptu group hug at the back of the church before they made their way down the aisle one at a time with their groomsmen partners.

Michael stood at the foot of the altar in his tux, smiling. When she reached him, together they ascended the steps where Father Pat, who had come up from Florida to conduct the ceremony, greeted them in the festive garments he wore for this occasion.

As time for a homily approached, Father Pat signaled to Peggy, and she picked up on his cue.

She stepped to the pulpit, where she thanked everyone for coming, including the friends of her parents who had traveled from Washington.

"This is a day of celebration for Michael and me, but I want to take this occasion to talk about my mom and dad.

"My parents created an Anniversary Box. The idea sprang from the pain they experienced as a young couple during a time when they struggled. Forces threatened to break them apart, egos dominated, and they were poised to throw everything away.

"But what prompted them to catch themselves? What stops us from throwing love away when we've been hurt by the one we love? How do we catch ourselves before we choose to walk away? And how do we repair the union? Then, how do we create a relationship that will be strong where it had been broken?

"My parents had a rocky start, but they chose to grow. They created an Anniversary Box, a tradition whereby each year, they would express something new that made them stronger as a couple. I wanted to find their stories so I could use them as a guide to create success in my own marriage.

"What makes love blossom and how do we keep the bloom on the rose alive? That is the question. How do we make love last forever?

"My parents lived by a simple theme. They called it: "one plus one equals one." For twenty-four years, on each anniversary, they would write a message together to reflect the principle that marriage is a journey to become one. My mom passed away shortly before their twenty-fifth anniversary, that golden milestone, but my dad wrote something to crystallize the significance of all they had built together.

"He wrote a letter, 'Number 25,' and put it into the Anniversary Box after my mom passed away. He wrote this letter only weeks before he had a stroke."

She removed the letter from its envelope and handed it to Father Pat who stepped to the microphone as she stepped back.

"I am happy to report that doctors feel confident that Peggy's dad, my cousin, Declan, will be strong enough, after his recent setback, to participate in a medication trial we all hope will move him forward," he said. "We're very thankful for that, so today, instead of a homily, I'd like to read the letter Declan wrote to Joan. His letter offers a powerful message on how to love in modern times."

Sweetheart.

I remember our first road race together as a couple, a 10K. I was faster than you in those days, and you waved me ahead. I finished before you, but at the finish line, I looked around and I could not find you. I got nervous, and I ran back out onto the course, searching, but no luck.

Then I saw you coming from the other direction. I hurried to you to ask what had happened, and you said you had taken a wrong turn. You ended up running double the distance, but you said it was fun just to be in the race with me. I asked you what you meant, and you said, 'You go as far as you can, for as long as you can, and you make it fun.'

That was the moment I fell in love with you, because I realized that's how you saw the world. You go as far as you can, for as long as you can, and you fill your life with love to make the 'going' fun.

Oh, we created memories of fun and love along the way. Remember? Each spring, we would drive back east from Oregon where I was in grad school to run in the Boston Marathon. One evening, as we drove through Montana heading to Boston with the sun setting behind us, we stopped to pick up a pizza and beer at a grocery store. You grabbed a six-pack of Coors, and we drove a while further until we found a campground. We pitched our tent and built a fire, and we sat around the fire to eat the pizza, warming it on the fire with tin foil, and we drank our Coors beer.

We laughed as darkness enveloped us and all was quiet in the mountain night but for the chirping of crickets and the popping of sparks from the fire as we looked into each other's eyes.

Coors beer and pizza. It became our short-hand for connecting completely. Love is the desire to learn everything about the other person. We resolved that night that we would support each other, that we would always want the best for each other, even if sometimes that became inconvenient, and we promised to remain by each other's side all the way through.

As we stared at the stars in the Montana sky, we picked out the North Star and we committed to each other to let our hearts be our North Star.

Many years later, when you got sick, we were about to head to Seattle for what we knew would be our last trip. You were slipping fast after fighting the lung cancer for four years, and the doctor called to recommend against driving to Seattle. I put you back in bed, and I prayed the new round of meds the doctor prescribed would take away your pain. As you lay in bed over the next few days, I leaned in close to you. Your breathing had become labored, and most times, your eyes were closed, but you opened them for me, and I saw you smile.

'How you doin?' I asked, and you said, barely above a whisper, 'Coors beer and pizza.'

Those would be the last words you spoke to me before the meds took over and sent you into a deep slumber. As I slept beside you that night, listening as your breathing grew shallow, my heart ached, not knowing if you were suffering, but I was so grateful to know that the memories we had created together were important to you.

The next day your breathing turned very faint, and that's when the hospice nurse who stopped by each morning to check on you told me the end was near. 'Go as far as you can for as long as you can.' I pulled up a chair beside the bed that morning, and I took your hand. I told you not to worry. We were in the last 385 yards of the marathon, and I was going to be with you all the way down the final stretch.

'I'm here,' I said. 'I'm not going anywhere.'

I held your hand all day, as the hours passed, and I told you your dad was in the room. 'He's watching,' I said. 'He's getting ready to take your hand.' And I could sense your face soften. A storm moved in. It shook the windows, and the lights flickered before the storm finally passed. Then it turned dark outside, and the only sound was the soft buzz of the light bulb in the lamp.

The nurse called to ask how you were doing, and I told her I could feel you slipping away. It was past midnight by that point, and she told me I needed to get some rest.

'This could go on a while longer,' she said. 'You need to be strong.'

I lay down beside you, and I closed my eyes for a moment, but soon I fell asleep, until I awakened with a start. It felt as if I had been jolted awake, and I felt a sense of lightness surrounding the bed. I could feel your presence hovering in the space above us, and I could sense a presence behind you, over your shoulder. It was your dad. He had come to take your hand, and I heard you say to him, 'Wait, we have to wake Declan before we go.'

It was you who woke me. I know you did. You woke me to say goodbye. You never would have left without saying goodbye. I could feel your lightness as you lingered another moment, and then I knew you were not suffering any longer — with your dad behind you. And then you were gone, the two of you, and I was alone.

All was still in the room. Everything was quiet, oh so very quiet. The hospice nurse had given me a number to call, and two men came. It was dark outside, and the *room was dimly lit. They spoke in whispers, as I stood in the doorway and watched them put you in their vehicle. One of the men saw me crying in the doorway, and he walked over to me and touched my arm.*

'Don't worry, we'll take good care of her,' he said, and I was so grateful for his kindness.

I watched their vehicle drive off until it turned the corner at the top of the block, and then it was gone. All was empty on the street in the dark and the quiet of the night, as I stood alone in the doorway. But I knew I was not alone, because I could feel you traveling in spirit right beside me. From the moment the vehicle turned the corner until now, I know you did not leave, and you have never left.

You have never gone away.

The church was silent, and all was still. The only sound came from the soft swoosh of the ceiling fans overhead. Gently, Father Pat folded the pages of the letter and slid them back into the envelope. He handed it to Peggy who stepped to the microphone again.

"That is the message," she said after a long pause. "That is the secret of 'one plus one equals one.' The Gift of the Magi Principle. When we give fully to each other, and do it simultaneously, we are joined forever.

"I wanted to know how the bond we create with someone can be made so strong that nothing can break it. I learned the secret from my parents. Two people start with an agreement to build on the foundation of everything good they've built in their relationship, then together, without prompting, they commit to meet each other's needs, as inconvenient as that might be at times.

"That's what the couple in the story, 'The Gift of the Magi,' did. The wife bought the chain for her husband, and he bought combs for her. They became one in that moment.

"Marriage is a journey to become one by learning

how to focus on what's most valuable to the other. That's the power that propels a relationship forward. We tap into that power when we give selflessly to each other.

"When we embrace each other fully, and do it simultaneously, even after one is gone, one plus one still equals one.

"We may feel alone at times, but we are not. We can know that the other is by our side, running stride for stride with us, clearing obstacles, shining a light to show the way.

"That's the Gift of the Magi Principle: when couples commit to the principle of one plus one equals one, their bond endures forever."

Chapter Twelve

Father Pat led Peggy and Michael through a recitation of their vows and the sharing of rings before he pronounced them man and wife. Then he turned them toward the crowd, which gave them a rousing burst of applause.

Miles away in a hospital, a nurse held up a phone for her father.

"Your daughter wanted me to stream this for you," she said.

The crowd in the church continued to clap as Peggy and Michael walked down the aisle heading for the door of the church. Strains of organ music filled the air and cameras flashed. They stepped out onto the steps in front of the church to more applause and handfuls of rice coming from all directions.

The wedding planner directed them to a waiting limo, where a series of cars lined up to take them and the wedding party—including the bridesmaids carrying fur coats on their arms—to a park around the corner for photos.

The bridesmaids formed a semi-circle under a big tree, all wearing their waist-length fur coats over their powder-blue dresses. Peggy took her place in the middle of the group, standing next to Kimberly who squeezed Peggy's hand. On cue, the group adopted stern expressions and hitched up a corner of their dresses to show some leg, and then laughed as the photographer clicked away.

Next, the photographer gestured to Peggy and Michael to follow him to a section of the park where he could frame them with the sunset as a backdrop. He positioned them so the fiery sky erupted like a rocket burst behind them, then as the photographer prepared to take the picture, Michael touched Peggy's hand.

"What?"

"I have something for you."

She looked down, and he had a golf ball in his hand. It was a Titleist 1.

"Titleist 1? What happened to Titleist 2?"

"One plus one equals one."

She smiled as she took the golf ball, then she signaled to one of her bridesmaids who carried her purse and handed it to her as if on cue. "And I have something for you."

"What?" he said.

She opened the purse and gave him the section of hose she had retrieved from the wastebasket at home.

"I'm giving you a mulligan, pal."

"Hah!" he laughed and he pulled the hose taut so she could see he was making a straight line with it. "Refresh my memory. Love goes in which end, and what comes out the other?"

"You're crazytown."

"Crazytown about you."

"Thanks for what you did for my dad, Michael."

"And thanks for what you did for me with Mickelson."

"I think we know the way home now, don't we?"

"Find the North Star, then use our hearts and minds to think and feel our way."

They gave each other fist bumps, like two magnets clicking.

"Okay, Peggy and Michael," said the photographer. "Over here please — look at me now, turn this way, smile. At the same time."

"Yes," they said, simultaneously.

The photographer took the shot, and the sunset picture became their formal wedding photo, with its symbolism of one day closing out and the promise of sunrise and a new day just ahead.

Several friends pointed out, however, that though perfect for a silver frame on the mantle, the photo left an opening for the grandkids to one day say: "So, what's with the golf ball and the hose?"

Epilogue

Peggy gave each of her bridesmaids a wooden Anniversary Box, a replica of her parents' box, with a rose on the front and the message: one plus one equals one.

Inside the box, she provided copies of the twenty-four Anniversary Box messages her parents had created together.

Her handwritten note to each person said, "Use these messages as a guide, but write your own messages together to affirm your bond. Write a new resolution each year. Then when you're old, you can look back over your years together to see how strong your union has become — and know it will endure forever for the investment you have made in each other along the way."

1. Build on what you've built.

The grass is not greener on the other side. At times, when our egos conspire to pull us apart, we will look to the "good" in our relationship and affirm that value. We will strive to build on the "good" and make it stronger. Strong begets strong!

2. It takes two to make "one" work.

Once we have determined the value in "us," we will strive to see each other's point of view. Even when we don't agree, we will work to understand each other. It takes two to make "one" work.

3. Not me, we!

There is nothing more powerful than two individuals who maintain their identities and yet agree to sublimate themselves when necessary to support each other's needs willingly. One plus one equals one.

4. Love means saying you're sorry.

"I'm sorry" are two powerful words. They take ownership of accountability and embrace vulnerability. We won't be afraid to say them to each other.

5. When you win, I win.

I want the best for you, even if sometimes that's not the best for me.

6. Do you want to be right, or do you want to be happy?

Marriage is the condition of compromise. We each don't have to be right all the time, and conceding a point can be a lovely gift. We will strive to give each other those gifts.

7. Coors beer and pizza.

We will tell each other what we like about each other, what our goals are, what's in our hearts. We will never stop being curious about ways to support each other, and we will strive to make "us" stronger in the context of conversation with beer or wine — and pizza, of course.

8. Right a wrong.

When one of us makes a mistake, we will be willing to admit it. And then, willing to fix it.

(See Number 4!)

9. Never play at being a victim.

Don't use passive aggression to get what you want. And if one of us does, we will resolve not to do it again.

10. Always tell the truth — but be discreet.

Some things are private. We won't ask each other to share everything about our pasts. The ability to live with ambiguity is next to godliness.

11. Water the rose.

Never take love for granted, and try to make each other feel special every day. Keep the bloom on the rose, that is the goal. We will work together to keep our love fresh and new.

12. Please and thank you.

'Nuff said.

13. High touch, high talk.

We will strive to satisfy each other sexually, but also strive to connect in conversation with equal passion.

14. Adversity is a worthy teacher — listen to the teacher.

We were not put on this earth to have it easy. We

will look at tough times as opportunities to build character and create a stronger union together.

15. Never bet against my baby!

The world may throw obstacles at us, but I will always be in your corner. Count on me!

16. Forgiveness is divine — and wise.

Anger hurts the one who holds on to their bitterness. Forgiveness is not about letting the other person off the hook, forgiveness is about setting ourselves free from the tightness that corrodes our spirit.

17. Go ahead, sing in the shower.

Who cares if I have no talent? I will sing. And that goes for dancing, too. (Both apply to Declan, not to Joan, haha.)

18. Run without a watch.

We will savor opportunities to move together through the woods or along a beach. We won't need a device to measure how far we've gone or tell us how long we've been out there. Moving together, sharing the experience, is our purpose.

19. Be uncommonly kind.

When someone comes up to either one of us with

a need, and one of us wants to help that person, the other will trust that the one who wants to help knows what they are doing.

20. Bills are our common foe — we are not foes.

It's no fun to get hit with big expenses, but when that happens, we will not fight. We will tackle bills together. (See also Number 14.)

21. Fire no shot in anger.

I will avoid saying anything in the heat of emotion that, with a cooler head, I may wish I could take back. Some hurtful things once said, last forever. (I will repeat this sentence until I truly get it!)

22. Some guys need a wedgie!

Nice as we may try to be with people, some may try to take advantage of our goodwill. If a guy needs a wedgie, we'll give him one, baby, together!

23. Tell me what you need.

Don't beat around the bush. Tell me what you need, then put the onus on me to deliver.

24. We may never pass this way again.

Marriage is not a destination. Marriage is a journey. We will search for moments to share, then we will celebrate the memories.

25. The Gift of the Magi Principle.

True love lasts forever.

About The Author

Tom Murphy has published three other books. In 2006, he wrote "Reclaiming the Sky," a story about the aviation heroes of 9/11, and founded the Human Resiliency Institute at Fordham University in New York to put healing lessons from the book into action. The lead program, Edge4Vets, teaches veterans how to tap their resiliency strengths to get jobs. See edge4vets.org.

In 2018, he followed up on a history of the Boston Marathon he co-wrote with Boston Marathon winner John J. Kelley, "Just Call Me Jock," with a Boston Marathon mystery novel, "Runner in Red" (Encircle Publications.) That story, based on a real-life Boston Marathon legend, follows a Boston TV reporter and former marathon champion as she searches for the first woman to run a marathon in America. Tom created a 5K race series based on the story to raise funds to cure lung cancer in memory of his wife, Barb, a marathon runner, who passed away from lung cancer. See runnerinred.com. In addition to the race series, he created a charity beer, Barb's Beer, to raise funds for the cause. See barbsbeer.org.

Tom has a B.A. from the University of Wisconsin and an MFA in Creative Writing from the University of British Columbia in Vancouver. He commutes between Boston and New York City.

He'll be introducing a "roundtable" discussion series to give people a chance to match "messages" in The Anniversary Box to strengths in their lives and in their relationships.

He'll be introducing a workshop series to teach people how to create their own Anniversary Box. The sessions will give readers a chance to match "messages" in the story to strengths in their lives.

To contact Tom, visit theanniversarybox.com.

CPSIA information can be obtained
at www.ICGtesting.com
Printed in the USA
FSHW021838090721
83103FS